BU

"I think I need to move to Alaska... Seriously though, Kelly Underwood did a wonderful job with this page-turner. I truly enjoyed getting to know the mysterious Grizz and meeting Dani a tenacious reporter that doesn't know the word quit. They learn to trust one another but ultimately God in this fast-paced action with the perfect amount of romance story."

—KATE, GOODREADS

"*Burning Truth* is a heart-pounding, adventurous read that has surprises, danger, action, and romance. Grizz and Dani have their own baggage from their past—trying to meet and live up to a parent's expectations, trust issues, and both felt like they had failed someone before. Such an exciting suspenseful read."

—ALLYSON, GOODREADS

"I am captivated by this series! Each one features more of the hotshots and smoke jumpers as they battle fires and domestic terrorists, and sometimes their past and their faith. I highly recommend *Burning Truth* and the entire Chasing Fire Alaska series for lovers of inspirational, non stop action, sweet romantic suspense stories."

—JEANNE, GOODREADS

"These stories continue to captivate me! I feel like I am a part of the hotshot team. I am eager for the next book to see how the story ends but will miss Alaska and all of these adventures."

BURNING TRUTH

CHASING FIRE ALASKA | BOOK 5

BURNING TRUTH

KELLY UNDERWOOD

sunrise
PUBLISHING

Burning Truth
Chasing Fire: Alaska, Book 5

Copyright © 2025 Sunrise Media Group LLC
Print ISBN: 978-1-966463-02-3

This book is a work of fiction. Names, characters, places, and incidents are either products of the author's imagination or used fictitiously. Any similarity to actual people, organizations, and/or events is purely coincidental. All Scripture quotations, unless otherwise indicated, are taken from the The ESV® Bible (The Holy Bible, English Standard Version®), © 2001 by Crossway, a publishing ministry of Good News Publishers. Used by permission. All rights reserved.

Additional Scripture quotations are taken from the Holy Bible, New International Version®, NIV®. Copyright ©1973, 1978, 1984, 2011 by Biblica, Inc.™ Used by permission of Zondervan. All rights reserved worldwide. The "NIV" and "New International Version" are trademarks registered in the United States Patent and Trademark Office by Biblica, Inc.™

For more information about the author, please access her website at kellyunderwoodauthor.com.

Published in the United States of America.
Cover Design: Sunrise Media Group LLC

· CHASING FIRE ALASKA ·

This book is dedicated to the real heroes: our first responders. To the men and women with police and fire departments all over the country who put their lives on the line every day for us to sleep in peace at night. I might write stories, but these men and women are the real deal.

With man this is impossible, but with God all things are possible.

MATTHEW 19:26 ESV

ONE

REPORTER DANI BARLOWE WASN'T sure which was worse—facing down an actual bear in the wilds of Alaska or duking it out with a pompous, gruff, grouchy hotshot aptly named Grizz.

After this, she was going to change her title to Adventure Reporter, because this was three thousand miles outside of her comfort zone.

She let out a huff that puffed up her blonde bangs. "This trip would have been so much easier if that hotshot crew hadn't thrown us out of their compound." Dani shoved a branch out of her way and trudged forward, her white boots sticking in the mud from the dirt trail. "How much farther is it, anyway?"

Josh Whitlock, the only man brave enough to

volunteer to be her cameraman and videographer on this escapade into the wilderness, trailed behind Dani. "Yeah, they weren't the friendliest. But according to the hand-drawn map your source gave you, we need to hike about a mile and a half, right? And are you actually going to tell me who your source is before the case is over?"

Dani ignored the sarcasm-laced comment and took the crinkled paper from Josh. No one could know that a local FBI agent, the husband of a friend of hers, had given a reporter information about an investigation he'd been forced to close.

Why was she sweating under her three layers? Wasn't Alaska supposed to be freezing? But at four p.m., the sun lit the mountain up in bright hues of red and orange with no signs of setting, and her Apple Watch indicated the temperature was sixty degrees.

"My source is one-hundred-percent legit." Skye had passed on the map just last week, explaining that two of her friends, Crew and JoJo, had flown a drone around after trail cameras had spotted unusual militia activity in this area.

They were here.

Wherever here was.

She rotated the map, and Josh chuckled from behind her.

Why were his broken-in boots barely muddy? He didn't have any rips in the sleeves of his company-issued windbreaker from the thorny branches, while her thick International News Network navy jacket looked like it had been shredded by wolves. "We just need to keep going . . . up. Once this muddy trail ends, we should find another pathway that takes us to the secret compound." Dani moved a tree branch out of the way and continued the hike. Josh's exaggerated sigh spurred her forward.

He didn't get her. At forty-six, Josh was fifteen years older than her and on the fast track to early retirement. The man was a perpetual bachelor who loved the comforts of home, while Dani was willing to do whatever it took for the sake of the story. But neither of them was cut out for this little adventure.

Which only made her press on—or up. She wasn't a quitter. There was no turning back now. Her mind had already churned out the sound bites for her special report.

Dangerous militia group hiding in middle-of-nowhere Alaska. Secret laboratory rumored to be tucked into the side of Copper Mountain.

All of it added up to her last shot at reviving her career.

Maybe if she was the one who broke this story first, the public would forget about the one time she'd had the facts completely wrong.

Her career as an investigative reporter for the International News Network had taken a nosedive three years ago after she'd botched a story accusing Alaskan senator Geoff Deville of embezzlement. Her intel had been solid, but when the judicial system had found him innocent, the court of public opinion had turned on her like a piranha, shredding her reputation. She'd clawed her way back to the top to regain the trust of viewers. Barely.

No way was she going to give up. Not when she'd come all this way to find a new story.

Not that she'd ever give up on proving Deville wasn't entirely innocent of wrongdoing. The man had a shady past, and if he stepped out of line, Dani would pounce.

She shimmied out of her jacket, tied it around her waist, and marched forward. "I trust my contact. There's a compound or a secret laboratory tucked away in these quiet mountains. I can smell it."

Josh grunted. "That's just how fresh air smells. Something you're not familiar with, living in Washington, DC. When's the last time you even went to a park or did anything outside? What did that hotshot call you?"

Diva Dani.

Why had they stopped at the Midnight Sun base camp first anyway? All she'd wanted to do was connect with her old friend, smokejumper Skye Parker, before following up on the information Skye and her husband, FBI Agent Rio Parker, had sent her. Instead, Dani had ended up facing off with a bunch of cranky hotshots.

One in particular had made her blood boil.

Grizz.

The man certainly resembled a grizzly bear, with his dark-brown shaggy hair, a bushy beard, thick shoulders, and that lumberjack T-shirt with the hotshot logo that stretched across his chest and showed off every one of his rippling muscles.

Get your head in the game, Barlowe.

Something about this thin mountain air had short-circuited her brain.

"Look." Dani turned toward Josh, but her feet wouldn't move. Her designer boots made a sucking sound with each mud-filled step. Josh grabbed her arm to steady her so she could free herself from the guck.

She shook the memories of the hotshots from her mind. If she wanted to come out on top, she had to put in the hard work now. It was up to her to make things happen. No one was showing up to help her save her career. Not her family, friends, or even God. Josh was only here for the overtime. People had showed their true colors the moment Dani's reporter status had soured and she wasn't the media darling anymore.

No. Second place wasn't an option for her.

She shook from Josh's grasp on her arm and trudged forward. "We'll make it there and back before dark, no problem. I've run a marathon before. How hard is a mile-and-a-half hike through the woods?"

Josh snorted. "Not that I want to agree with that hotshot—what was his name? Grizz? But are you sure you're good in those boots?"

She looked down at her once-white fluffy ski boots, now brown and caked with dirt. "Well, I figured if they were good enough for skiing, they'd be fine for Alaska."

What did she know about hiking, or skiing for that matter? She was more of an indoorsy girl. Maybe she should have done better research before booking the first flight out of DC after getting this lead.

Dani tucked fallen strands of her shoulder-length blonde hair back under her multicolor knit cap. "I can't believe you're taking that Neanderthal's side. That guy was the definition of *backwoods*. I can't believe he said we had a death wish. So insufferable. He practically yelled at us."

It almost seemed like Alaskan Mountain Man had gotten under her skin.

No, she wouldn't let that happen. Even if the guy was her type, relationships were just a distraction. She needed to focus on increasing her public approval ratings.

Dani shoved another tree branch out of her way only for it to whip back into her face. Who lived like this?

She looked around and saw nothing but brown and dark-green foliage. No noises except some buzzing insects or an occasional chirping bird. Her apartment in DC had all the modern conveniences a person wanted. But this? They were miles from that general store and restaurant they'd passed on the way up the mountain.

"Admit it, Dani, you're out of your element. There's no shame in us turning around. Especially when your lead is based on a rumor. The government isn't even investigating this claim. Maybe we should just return to the hotshot base and wait for your friend to return."

Without this story, she had nothing left. Her

boss had read her the riot act. *Don't bother returning unless you have the story.*

She tamped down her frustration and kept walking. "Something's going on in these woods, and we're going to be the first to report it."

"Not sure it's worth risking my life."

"You can quit if you want, Josh. Go back and tell stories by the campfire with those hotshots. But I'm going to find out what's happening with this secret lab in the woods. What if it's a terrorist camp? We need to expose it so someone will investigate."

He shook his head. "The hotshots wouldn't give us the time of day. Not after our station roasted them on air. I don't want to face them again."

On the inside, Dani let out a sigh of relief.

She remembered the scathing story her station had run. It'd been a low blow when the hotshots had refused to take them to the location. She should have called ahead to make sure Skye was available this morning. They'd been friends since college, so when Rio's investigation had been stonewalled, he'd had Skye feed her information about this dangerous group in the hope Dani could break the story wide open. Too bad the smokejumpers had been out fighting a fire when she and Josh had arrived. Instead of seeing Skye and letting her know Dani was on the case, they'd been shown the door.

She refused to give up, even if it meant spending the night roughing it on the side of a mountain.

Which was exactly what those hotshots had predicted.

So what if she had a homemade map and zero outdoor survival skills? If she could swim in the Washington, DC fish tank of political piranhas, she could survive a mountain hike.

But hiking a mountain to an undisclosed location in the hopes of breaking a story?

Hold my extra-hot, sugar-free, oat milk latte . . . because this is where Dani Barlowe shines.

She pulled the map from her jacket pocket and studied it. A raindrop plopped on the paper, blurring the ink. She shielded it with her hand.

"Here's where we parked the car, at the entrance to the national park. And I see the end of the nature trail, which means we should find another pathway that takes us up the mountain. We're going to be just fine. You'll see."

As if to mock her, the Alaskan skies opened up, and rain soaked them. She shoved the map into her dry pocket, hoping it would stay protected.

After two and a half hours battling tree limbs, flooding, a deranged beaver, a snake, and an army of mosquitoes, they reached the end of the trail. The dirt path faded into overgrown shrubs and a wall of rocks.

Dani's pulse hammered in her ears. She hadn't come all this way to walk away with nothing. There had to be a second path to follow. So far, the map hadn't gotten them lost. "Look, there's a section of brush that's worn down. I bet this is the way."

Josh gaped at her. "Dani, I have a bad feeling about this."

She put her hands on her hips, her multiple layers of sweaters under her windbreaker making her arms look like the Stay Puft Marshmallow Man. Okay, so maybe she'd overdressed a bit, as indicated by the sweat rolling down her back. "Let's check this path, and if we don't find anything in a half hour, we'll turn around."

He nodded, but his pale face and huffed breath indicated he wasn't fully on board. At least he followed her through the narrow opening that led up. Just . . . up.

The rain intensified, and the trees provided minimal shelter from the deluge. She was soaked four layers deep. *Path* wasn't the correct term for their route. This was the definition of off-grid. No markings or any kind of directional signs. No signs of human life. Just some trampled earth that indicated hikers had at one point headed off the beaten path in this direction. Were they going to find anything on this deserted mountainside? And how long would it take to get back to civilization, anyway?

They trekked on without talking. Her labored breaths rattled around in her ears.

A buzzing sound stopped her dead in her tracks. At her abrupt stop, Josh bumped into her.

"What was that?" Dani whispered. But in the quiet of the mountainside, it sounded like she had a megaphone.

"Sounds man-made. Like electricity."

Her heart beat double time. This was it.

The mystery compound.

They crept through the branches and bushes. Adrenaline fueled Dani's feet, despite the ache in her calves from the mountain hike. She swept a tree limb out of her way and spotted a chain-link fence in the clearing below them, complete with razor-sharp barbed wire across the top.

"Whoa." Josh took his camera out of the bag and began filming. "What is this place?"

They ducked down and watched the valley

below. They were far enough away to not be spotted, but Dani didn't trust that one crackle of a tree branch underfoot wouldn't give away their hiding location.

At least they were higher than the camp and could see directly into it. Behind the fence were several buildings, camouflaged in brown and green colors. One of the huts was three times the size of the others, with what looked like steel doors and solid walls.

"Whatever this is, it can't be good." Josh stood beside her, surveying the scene below. His breath was heavy. From exertion or fear?

Dani couldn't respond. All she could do was take it in.

She'd found her story.

Movement inside the compound caught her attention. Two men in army fatigues came into view with M4 assault rifles slung over their shoulders. They dragged a man through the courtyard and into the middle of the compound.

Even from a distance, Dani could see the gray-haired man stumble, his once-white shirt tattered and stained with . . . blood?

"Get a close-up of their faces." A third man exited the building. "Especially that guy." Something about the man made Dani's insides quake.

He walked with an air of authority and barked orders to the other two men, although she couldn't hear what he was saying. But the man was definitely familiar. She'd examine the footage later.

One of the men opened the door to the main hut and dragged the prisoner inside, but not before Dani got a good look inside. "Josh, did you see that stack of weapons? Did you get a picture of it?" A rack of rocket launchers and guns along one wall.

Josh nodded, his eyes wide. "Who are these men?"

A knot tightened in the pit of Dani's stomach. "They may be part of a rebel group known as the Sons of Revolution. But that's a lot of firepower hidden in the side of a mountain."

She needed to get back to civilization in time to report her findings. With any luck, they could be on the air for the morning East Coast news.

Leaves crunched, and Dani turned to watch Josh back up ten steps, his eyes wide and his hands trembling around the camera. "I can't . . . we shouldn't be here. We've got enough footage. We need to leave."

"Wait. We need to see what's going on. Get more evidence. We need to stick together. Just thirty seconds more—"

Josh set the camera on a rock. "You stay. I'm leaving. With or without you. I'm not risking my life for a story. No job is worth this. Admit it, we're in over our heads."

A chimney puffed out white smoke—more like an industrial smokestack than a cozy fireplace.

A chill raced through Dani, and it wasn't because of the Alaska temperatures. According to Skye, SOR had been testing a biological weapon designed to poison food and water supplies. Fish and other animals in the area had died when exposed to the toxin. Skye's team had helped shut down SOR's base camp, had even destroyed their warehouse along with most of the toxin, but the toxin had to have been made somewhere.

Was that what was going on behind those walls? And why hadn't the FBI shut this group down?

She turned to tell Josh they needed to run in just a few seconds, but he was gone.

All she could hear was the pounding of her heart. There wasn't a person in sight for miles that could help her now that Josh had fled. The discarded camera perched on a stone was the only reminder that he'd been there a few seconds ago.

She looked over the ridge. These men were dangerous, and she was alone. She checked her phone and wanted to toss it down the mountain. No bars. She shoved it into her coat pocket.

How had her laser-focused reporter instincts derailed her so badly? Both Josh and Grizz had tried to warn her, but she hadn't listened.

She'd take Grizz's ornery nature in a heartbeat over her odds with militant men and a secret compound. Her mind went numb, and her hands wouldn't cooperate. Those men hadn't seen her. At least she could still collect evidence for the authorities. And her story that would inevitably follow.

Dani turned on the camera, hit record, and scanned the compound to document everything.

How was she going to get out of the woods? At least she had the map. It was still light outside, and it would be until late, surely. But would she be stuck hiking down the mountain in the dark anyway?

Don't panic. Do. not. panic.

A scream shredded the silence.

Dani froze with the camera rolling. She watched as the guards dragged another prisoner across the courtyard.

Not a prisoner.

The man had a windbreaker on, and Dani

could see the yellow INN logo calling to her like a beacon.

International News Network. Her network.

Josh.

What were they going to do to him?

She had to rescue her cameraman. But how? She looked around for a rock to throw or something she could use as a weapon. Maybe she could set off a distraction and give Josh time to run.

But then what? She wouldn't be able to fight these guys off when they inevitably came for her.

No weapons. No self-defense skills. No contact with the outside world.

Her legs gave out and she pitched forward, her knees hitting the dirt. Her breaths came short and fast, and she clutched her chest, willing her lungs to take in air.

The gunshot stopped her heart. Josh slumped to the dirt, and the men behind the fence turned to look at her.

Dani realized then that she'd screamed.

No no no. Adrenaline surged, and her brain shouted for her to run.

She sprinted through the woods, part of her trying to remain quiet while the other part shouted at her to pick up speed.

She tripped and dropped the camera.

No time to retrieve it. She righted herself and raced forward.

Behind her, a twig snapped. At this point, she prayed it was a bear.

Chancing a look over her shoulder, she saw a man through the tree branches. Make that two men. With big guns. She froze, but it didn't matter. They'd spotted her.

She bolted, tree limbs whipping her in the face. The mud from the rain made the terrain slippery, and she prayed her feet wouldn't fly out from under her. Down the mountain she went.

A bullet whizzed by her head. She clamped her mouth shut, but it didn't stop the scream that reverberated across the mountainside.

She was going to die on this mountain. And no one was coming to her rescue.

Grizz glanced at his watch for the third time. This unnecessary delay was cutting into his time off. He was out of here, as soon as Skye finished yelling at the crew.

"I don't care if Dani's station was the one that had that unflattering report about the hotshots. You should have helped her." Skye's voice bounced off the metal walls of the long rectangular building that doubled as their mess hall. He needed to get to the vehicle bay where he'd stashed his ATV. After working and living three months at base camp, Grizz couldn't wait to get back to his cabin.

"I can't believe you sent her away to climb Copper Mountain on her own." Skye glared at Mack, Hammer, Saxon, and Grizz individually. "You know we've had some flash flooding and mudslides from the rain."

This was not his first time being on the receiving end of a dressing down by someone who wasn't his superior. But they'd had it coming.

The Trouble Boys were in trouble. Again. And somehow, Grizz had gotten lumped in with them.

So maybe he could have stepped in and cut the glitzy woman some slack.

Nah.

Far as Grizz was concerned, that diva city reporter had no business hiking Copper Mountain to chase a rumor of a secret compound.

He'd never be able to protect someone so headstrong from the wilds of Alaska. Grizz had hung up his superhero cape long ago.

"In our defense," Mack said, "she didn't tell us she knew you. And you should have seen her outfit. All she needed was one of those teeny purse dogs and she would have rivaled a Kardashian."

Grizz looked to the big man standing next to him. Hammer, Mack's older brother, said nothing, leaving Mack to run his mouth. Saxon flanked the other side of Hammer, not bothering to insert himself in the discussion. Mack was the youngest of the group and had a lot to learn—although anyone under the age of twenty-five was a kid as far as Grizz was concerned. Sometimes it paid to stay quiet.

Three of the hotshots were ex-Army like him, but Grizz had never met Hammer, Saxon, or Kane while he was serving. He didn't know why they'd chosen wildland firefighting or why they'd brought Hammer's kid brother along. But he knew it had something to do with the female hotshot, Sanchez.

Wherever Sanchez was, that was where you could find Kane.

"What even is a Kardashian?" Hammer snickered. The tattoo across the man's thick forearm spelled *Trouble*. They all shared the blame in making snide comments about the fish-out-of-water guests, but no one was going to admit that to Skye.

Skye fixed her fists on her hips and glared at all of them. "So you let Dani and her cameraman wander into the woods alone?" Her beet-red face conveyed her anger, underscored by her sharp, overenunciated words. They all knew better than to mess with Skye, because no one wanted to tangle with her husband Rio if he caught wind of the situation. The FBI agent was well-connected, and Grizz refused to get on that man's bad side.

Grizz knew he'd been the worst offender. He'd more or less snarled at the beauty queen while the others laughed. "Her station is the one that called us the 'lukewarm shots' last year after we failed to stop a fire from ravaging a fancy new subdivision."

He'd seen that yellow network logo embroidered on her thick blazer, and it'd all rushed back.

But Skye had a valid point.

What could Grizz say to end this conversation? Skye was standing in the way of his time off. "Maybe we could have been more accommodating." Even if playing tour guide to a couple of clueless reporters wasn't in his official job description, he could have behaved better.

"Thanks, Grizz. I appreciate you volunteering to head out and find them."

Wait, what?

Skye wasn't his boss. Why was she giving the orders? He wasn't responsible for these two city slickers that'd wandered into base camp with some half-baked theory.

He bit back a growl. "How do you even know they're lost? I'm going to check on my cabin. We haven't had a night off in months!"

Skye's eyes looked like they might shoot laser beams and fry him where he stood.

"Fine." Grizz bit the words out. "I'll take my ATV and check on Dani and the cameraman. Make sure they're not bear chow."

Time to play nice and not let the surly mountain-man vibe win this round, despite everything within him wanting to retreat to his cabin. Alone.

Where he belonged.

Not that he didn't love his team. The hotshots had his back when putting out wildfires. But in general, he was skeptical of new people. Especially a nosey reporter sniffing out a story. Trust didn't come naturally to him. He'd been burned one too many times to let outsiders in.

It was even the reason he'd stopped going to church. How was he supposed to trust God when God had so many untrustworthy followers? Everyone had an angle to work.

Grizz watched the other hotshots scatter like raindrops. He'd check on the out-of-towners, but he wasn't getting involved in their drama. Not at all.

He grabbed his gear from his bunk room and

nodded his goodbyes to his team. He headed to the vehicle bay where he'd stashed one of his prize possessions—a red four-wheeled Raptor two-person ATV. Not that he ever shared his ride, but he loved the way the vehicle ate up the trails with its twenty-one-inch wheels. He cranked the motor and exited the garage only to be greeted with cold rain pelting his face.

Great. Skye was probably right to send him out here, even if it was miserable weather. That city girl and her boyfriend had no business being out in this rain, and it probably was his fault they were out alone.

Even with diminished visibility and slick, muddy ground, Grizz pressed on. He knew this mountain better than anyone. This was practically his backyard. His cabin was ten miles to the west, but for now, he'd head east and up the mountain trail. He hadn't expected the detour, but he had a full tank of gas, so he'd have plenty to make it to the cabin.

What had that reporter been thinking? As a hotshot, it was his job to protect the people who lived on the mountain, and their homes, from wildfires. If there was some rogue secret camp up here, Grizz and his team would have already spotted it.

Over the last few weeks, their smokejumpers had tangled with plenty of militia guys. Logan had rescued Jamie, a civilian, from a militia compound that had been burned by wildfire. The Feds had classified the information about the compound, so it was unlikely that a reporter from DC knew something Grizz's team didn't.

Cadee and Vince had found dead salmon out of season. Orion and Tori had been certain the militia had set up shop somewhere new.

If it was local to the Midnight Sun base, surely they'd know.

Despite the inclement weather, the temperatures were Alaska-perfect at sixty degrees. He wore his hotshot T-shirt and wondered if he should have changed into shorts before leaving.

Rain pelted him in the face as he drove the ATV along the winding paved trail, but he'd take the rain over the dry season that had sparked so many fires.

He laughed at the thought of Dani Barlowe in her puffy network blazer with fourteen layers underneath. Her station's story about the hotshots brought back all kinds of unpleasant memories. His team had failed to stop a wildfire from taking out a group of homes after it had blazed too close to civilization. No one had cared that the fire had been started by someone carelessly tossing a lit cigarette into the brush. All that'd mattered was that a celebrity's summer home had gone up in smoke along with other overpriced residences in a fancy new subdivision at the base of Copper Mountain. Suddenly the hotshots had been the villains, inept at their jobs.

It was bad enough that his team had failed, but had it needed to become an international scandal? The good guys never could win.

And that horrible nickname the station had imposed on them . . . *lukewarm shots*.

Even if she hadn't written the piece herself, she was guilty by association as far as he was concerned.

After fifteen minutes, Grizz pulled into the state park entrance. The area provided access to several hiking trails that circled Copper Mountain. One lone car sat in the empty parking lot. The same white Subaru Outback that Dani and the cameraman had driven to base camp.

The asphalt trail ended, and the main trail switched to a dirt path. What were these two up to? Had they made it this far? Grizz parked his vehicle up the hill from the parking lot and obscured it in some bushes to protect it from the rain. He pulled out his phone to call Skye with an update. No bars. It wouldn't be the first time a storm had knocked out communications on the mountain.

Grizz made his way to the trailhead. Had Dani made it up these steep hills covered with rocks and mud? He'd definitely underestimated the woman's tenacity if she had.

After thirty minutes, his calf muscles strained with each step. He paused to catch his breath when the dirt trail ended at a scenic photo stop.

Where was Dani?

Despite the rain, Grizz spotted a freshly trampled patch of brush that hadn't been washed away. It wasn't a marked trail, but Grizz had a feeling Dani and the cameraman had continued on, so he set out on foot, up the path beyond where most tourists and locals stopped hiking.

Grizz navigated through the trees and shrubs, climbing the steep slope of the mountain. How far had Dani and her friend hiked? What was so important to her that she'd make this treacherous climb?

He pushed another branch out of his way and froze. A strong, earthy smell hit his nose. The sound of water flowing rumbled close by.

It had the markings of a mudslide. The past few rainy days had taken a toll on the mountain.

A few minutes later, Grizz reached the spot where the water, mud, rocks, and debris flowed down the mountainside. It drifted by him and headed toward the road he'd taken in, which meant getting back to base would be treacherous. His ATV wouldn't handle mud in its engine.

He walked parallel to the flow of muck, looking for any signs of Dani and the cameraman.

A boulder interrupted the flow of the mudslide, which sent the river of dirt and debris around it. But Grizz saw the flash of yellow.

The INN logo.

A lifeless figure lay scrunched up against the rock, covered in mud.

He raced to the boulder and stepped through the muck to clear away some of the sludge. "Oh no no no."

Dani lay sprawled in the guck. He checked for breath and found a pulse. Her blonde hair stuck up at odd angles all around her pale face, but she was alive.

"Dani, can you hear me?"

A groan sent his heart soaring, but she didn't rouse. Her pulse was strong, and he didn't see any blood or injuries apart from the knot on her head that swelled beneath his fingers. Her dark-blonde eyelashes lay flat on high cheeks.

What had happened to her? And where was the cameraman?

The rain intensified.

After assessing her injuries, he deemed it safe to move her, so he hoisted her up and cradled her in his arms.

She never woke or even flinched.

Grizz headed back to his ATV, making each step deliberate so as not to slip. His head swiveled on alert, looking for danger but also for the man that had been with Dani. Where was the preppy one with the camera?

And how had she slipped and slid down the mountain in a mudslide?

He looked up the mountainside but didn't see anything alarming.

Then the hair on his arms rose, and Grizz's instincts all went on high alert.

Someone was watching them.

Dani still wasn't moving. Grizz made the decision to get her off the mountain and get help. As he hoisted her up in his arms, he craned his neck around the area. Where was the cameraman? He'd have to go back once he got Dani out of the pelting rain and made sure she was stable.

The mountain was too quiet, other than the trickle from the flowing mud. Grizz marched one foot in front of the other, each step planted firmly to keep from stumbling while carrying Dani.

The sound of a gunshot sent him sprinting down the mountain. Bark exploded from a tree in front of him, sending shards of wood flying.

This wasn't some hunter mistaking him for a caribou. Had Dani stumbled into something?

Grizz doubled his grip on the reporter and zigzagged his way down the trail, toward the ATV. He thought about taking her rental car but didn't have the keys . . . or time. Whoever was at the end of that high-powered rifle might give chase.

Grizz set Dani in the front of his ATV, sandwiched between him and the handlebars. Her head lolled to the side, and he wrapped his arm around her, letting her fall against his chest.

Not that he'd talked with God much lately, but he sent up a quick prayer that the trail hadn't washed out with the mudslide like he'd anticipated.

When he got to the narrow trail, it was filled with muck. Dani's SUV was sitting in the equivalent of swamp water. No way would her car make it down the only access road to civilization. At least he'd parked his ATV on higher ground.

"Just great." They were cut off from the main way up and down the mountain. Why would he expect God listen to him? Grizz had been radio silent for a long time.

The rain intensified, and Grizz pointed his ATV toward his cabin. A little farther up the mountain, he could pick up another paved trail that led home. He'd just have to off-road it for a bit. At least it would get them out of the rain and away from a shooter. Dani could be dry and warm when she woke up, and he could figure out a way to call for help.

The ATV wheels flicked dirt and mud behind him while his racing mind conjured up scenarios as to what had happened to the other guy—her friend.

After thirty minutes of navigating on and off the trail through the rain, Grizz parked the ATV and killed the motor.

Home sweet home.

He hadn't laid eyes on his cabin in a few months. Plenty of forest fires had kept his team round-the-clock busy.

The cabin lay on five acres of pristine forest nestled in the heart of Copper Mountain. The pine trees acted as a wall all around his cabin, offering protection with their thick branches and foliage. In the distance, several mountain peaks broke through the horizon. The cabin was Grizz's safe haven in the middle of the untamed, unspoiled wilderness. His nearest neighbor was the perfect distance of two miles away.

His grandfather had built the cabin when Grizz was young and left it to him when he passed away. Once Grizz had returned from serving in the Army, this had been the closest thing he'd had to a home.

With its espresso-colored wood-grain finish and wraparound porch, Grizz's place might not have all the modern amenities like some of the other monstrous summer homes rich people built farther down the mountain, but it was all his, complete with a few personal touches he'd added to the outhouse.

He smiled. Now, that was special—not a functioning outhouse like when his grandparents had lived here, but definitely very useful.

Grizz lifted Dani and carried her into his house—across the threshold, even though he wasn't the marrying kind and she wasn't the kind of woman for him. He couldn't wait to kick off his muddy boots and line them up under the hooks where he kept his winter gear. At home, he could be himself. Kick back, relax, yet still be on high alert.

If that shooter came looking for Dani, Grizz would be ready.

The main room consisted of a living room, complete with wood-burning stove in the right-hand corner, which heated the whole place in the winter, and a kitchen area on the left wall, where his grandmother's mustard-yellow refrigerator rattled and hummed. Probably nothing compared to Dani's expensive tastes. But Grizz took good care of his cabin after inheriting it from his grandparents.

He set her on his grandpa's denim-blue couch, covered her with a fleece blanket, and let out a deep breath. Her presence threw off the vibe of his cabin. Despite his love for his team, he rarely had any visitors to his place.

He strode across the room and tossed the useless phone with no bars on the circle dinette table that overlooked the front window, then sat to unlace his muddy boots.

Should he leave her here and hike to his neighbor? The guy was a medic. He might know how long it would take her to wake up.

But a scream answered his question.

Dani bolted upright, her eyes wild.

He took a step toward her, about to speak, when she screamed again.

"Stay away from me. Help!"

TWO

DANI SCRAMBLED UP OFF THE COUCH, her head pounding worse than anything she'd ever felt. Her thoughts... nowhere to be found. "Who... who are you?"

Her captor stared at her with both hands up but said nothing. He frowned. The big guy wore a T-shirt and jeans and had a thick, full beard. Did she like beards?

Who was this guy?

She backed up and patted her coat pockets with trembling fingers, hunting for any kind of weapon. Or did she own a phone? This man was going to kill her. And she wasn't going down without a fight.

The bearded lumberjack stood in the center of the room.

A living room? Where was she?

"I'm not going to hurt you." He had a warm voice, soft, but she just knew he could be loud if necessary. He said, "We met, remember? I'm Grizz. You stopped by base camp on the way up Copper Mountain."

"I don't know you." *Think, Dani, think.* "Where am I? Why did you take me?"

The big guy took two steps closer, and she shrank back until she hit a wall beside the door. Could she make a run for it? Would this grizzly bear of a man chase her?

"No one is going to hurt you, Dani." He stopped moving. "You were in trouble, and I got you to safety. This is my cabin. In Alaska."

Alaska? She lived in Washington, DC.

How had she wound up five time zones away?

Dani didn't know much about him or what was happening, but she did know that she was an investigative journalist. As such, she'd get to the bottom of this story. Just as soon as her insides stopped quaking. She patted all of her pockets but couldn't find her cell phone. She definitely had a phone. But where was it?

And who would she even call?

"Did I have a cell phone on me?" Why had she asked? Like this guy would tell her the truth.

He shook his head. "Sorry, I didn't see one. You slid down the mountain in a mudslide, so you may have dropped it."

Grizz stomped to the kitchen on the opposite side of the cabin, each footstep pounding in sync with Dani's headache. "I'm going to make us some soup."

The Midnight Sun hotshot logo on his T-shirt stretched across the man's chest. *Hotshot?*

Her mind scrambled for memories. Sounds of laughter haunted her. And someone calling her a diva?

She sank to the dusty wood floor, her back skidding down the wall. She needed to keep this guy talking. "What happened when you saw me? I don't remember."

He pulled a container out of the freezer and dumped the frozen contents into a pot. A blue flame from the stove glowed. He stirred the meal with a wooden spoon. "I'm a Midnight Sun hot-shot. You and another man came into our base camp asking about some sort of secret compound in the woods. We advised you against traipsing up the mountain by yourselves, but you headed out anyway."

"I was working on a story," she whispered. "My—my boss encouraged me to follow a lead I got from an inside source here in Alaska. He gave me an ultimatum. I had to get the story."

Grizz turned toward her, interest in his eyes.

She'd said too much.

She closed her eyes, and an image of Josh popped into her head. The sound of a gunshot reverberated, and she saw him fall. In her mind—her memories. Her eyes sprang open. "Where's Josh? He was with me. You just told me he arrived when I did."

Grizz ladled some soup into a mug and placed it on an end table by the couch. He held out his hand to her. "Come sit on the couch and have some soup."

She complied, mainly because her stomach let out a gurgle as if to prove the man's point.

"Fine." But she waved off his hand and stood on her own. She sank onto the plush sofa, which was pretty nice for a bachelor pad. At least, she assumed the mountain man wasn't married. The place lacked throw pillows or homey décor. But it was warm, dry, and immaculate.

She took the mug of soup and wrapped her hands around the warm stoneware. He sat down at the other end of the couch. "I don't know where

Josh is. You were caught in a mudslide and hit a rock. You probably bumped your head when you tumbled down the mountain and crashed into that boulder."

She ran a hand through her hair and felt the knot on her temple. "Josh. He's still out there?"

This was her story, and she remembered talking Josh into going with her. Now he was missing?

Grizz met her eyes. "Look, I don't know what you found when you and Josh hiked up Copper Mountain, but given how I found you, I think he's in trouble."

"We have to go search for him." She tried to stand, but her legs betrayed her, and she ended up on the couch again.

Grizz looked out the front picture window, where fat drops pelted the glass. "The rain is getting worse. It must have knocked out a cell tower, because I have no signal here. I promise, we'll go look for Josh once this storm slows down. Right now, visibility is zero."

"Why should I trust you?" She took a spoonful of the soup, then downed the whole mug. When was the last time she'd eaten?

He sipped the soup. "Because I'm Grizz. We've met."

She set the mug down on the end table—which

was basically a repurposed tree stump—refusing to admit the soup had made her head quit pounding so much.

"You live here alone?" She nodded to the living room, complete with exposed wood beams and bare walls. She half expected a moose head to grace the mantel over the fireplace, but the decorations were minimal.

"I do. I spend a lot of time at base camp, but this place belonged to my grandparents, and after they passed away, I fixed it up and stay here when I'm not at base camp."

She squinted as she listened to the man's deep, gravelly voice. Fuzzy images parked themselves just out of reach. They had met.

All she remembered about their encounter was this man's gruff demeanor. "Is Grizz your first or last name? Or a nickname?"

He chugged the remnants of the soup from the mug and wiped his mouth with the back of his hand. Flecks of broth bits littered his beard. "Grizz is my last name."

"Do I get a first name?"

He shook his head. "No one knows my first name. And if they do, they don't dare say it."

She snorted. "I can see why you go by Grizz. You're meaner than a grizzly bear."

He walked over to her and invaded her space. She recoiled. He stooped, collecting her mug while meeting her at eye level. "Really? Have you ever come face-to-face with a grizzly bear before?"

He backed off and headed to the kitchen before she could form a sarcastic retort.

Have you met a bathtub and razor before?

Oh yeah, that was a good one. But probably best not to poke the bear-man. She looked down at her own mud-crusted attire and cringed. She was one to judge. Her INN jacket had a tear, and why was she wearing white—now brown—boots?

Grizz had busied himself in the kitchen area, which was basically a refrigerator and the two-burner stove. Did the man have a coffee maker? No way could she live this primitively.

Her stomach gurgled, and she prayed he hadn't heard.

"Grizz. I need to use a bathroom."

He pointed to the front door, the beginning of a smile on his face. "Outhouse. Turn left at the fallen tree. Grab some leaves on the way for TP. Oh, and take a flashlight to scare the coyotes away. They don't like the light."

No. Just no.

An outhouse? With coyotes. "I've woken up in a nightmare."

Grizz had the audacity to laugh at her.

She stood and moved toward the back window. There was no hope for that man. Clouds hung low in the sky, heavy with yet more rain, and she had no idea what time it was. Outside, there was a tiny shack on the side of the mountain.

He wasn't kidding. And she really needed to use the facilities, however primitive and scary they were.

"Okay. I can do this." She pulled her jacket tight around her and headed for the front door.

"Wait. I'm kidding. I mean, the house has an original outhouse, but it's not what you think. I have two bedrooms and a bathroom at the back, with working plumbing. Here, I'll show you."

She followed him down a hallway that led to two bedrooms, the window at the end overlooking the forest. Grizz's place was tucked up against the side of a mountain, so the view was trees and not much else. But it made the place feel cozy.

Warm. Safe.

He lumbered to the kitchen, and she used the restroom, surprised at how clean and fairly modern it was. It was possible that in her disorientation, and with a pounding headache, she might've been a smidge unfair in judging this man and his simple life.

A claw-foot tub with a big chip on the rim looked like it had been there for decades. The idea of sinking into hot water and getting cleaned beckoned her in a way that made her nearly whimper. But she needed to get off this mountain and away from the distracting man who had a fancy tub in his remote cabin in the middle of nowhere and made delicious soup. She needed to focus and find Josh.

She washed her face in the sink, then used a washcloth from the cupboard underneath to wipe the chunks of mud and dried blood from her hair. She looked in the mirror at her flushed face, and one blurry memory surfaced.

Diva Dani. That's what Grizz had called her.

Oh, she'd show him the real Dani—the one that never gave up. Just as soon as she could think straight and find her way in a rainstorm, she would get out of here and search for Josh.

By herself.

Dani slipped into the room next to the bathroom, which looked like Grizz's bedroom. Again, no decorations, just a basic black comforter covering the king-size bed.

Hang on a second. There was something tacked to the wall. Not art.

A bow.

Must be for hunting. Hanging next to it was a bag full of arrows.

She took the bow off the wall and grabbed an arrow. So she'd never even held a bow before, but at least it was a weapon.

She peered out the door of the bedroom and caught a glimpse of Grizz in the kitchen. The smell of coffee hit her, and her stomach rumbled again. But there wasn't time for luxuries.

Her memory might have failed her, but she knew Josh was in trouble.

Dani grabbed the bow and slung it over her shoulder, along with the bag of arrows. The bedroom window opened without so much as a squeak, and she climbed out. She couldn't trust the mountain man she vaguely remembered to save the day.

She needed to find Josh.

This reporter was going to be the death of him.

He had sensors on his doors and windows and knew the instant she'd opened the bedroom window. His closed-circuit security system let out a chime, indicating that he had a runner on his hands.

She had grit, that was for sure. The reporter wasn't going down without a fight, and he liked that in a woman.

In Alaska, it was about the only way a person survived.

If only he could erase that fear in her eyes when she looked at him. He wasn't the bad guy.

He walked out the front door and toward the rear of the cabin. And ran smack into Dani rounding the corner of the house.

"Wh-what are you doing?" She took two steps back with the bow in her arms. She had an arrow in place and pulled on the string. Too bad the arrow was pointing the wrong way. He stifled a smile. She was cute and dangerous at the same time. She'd get them both killed if she ran off on her own. Because he'd follow her.

"I'll shoot you. Don't think I won't."

At her faux bravery, his heart thawed a little bit toward his unwanted guest. "If you do, you'll shoot the tree behind you and hurt yourself." He walked up to her and flipped the arrow around. "If you want to leave, I'm not stopping you. But you'll need a weapon you can handle."

She lowered the bow. "Like what?"

Evidently, the key to this woman was to keep her intrigued.

He pulled his switchblade out of his pocket and passed it to her. She turned it around in her palm. "Just don't stab me in the back. But it might make you feel better to have a way to defend yourself."

He went around the front and headed inside to grab two cups of coffee. He met her on the wraparound porch outside the front door.

She dropped the bow and watched him, still clutching the pocketknife. He passed her a cup of coffee and offered her a seat in one of the two rocking chairs that were his favorite spot on the mountainside.

She tucked the knife into her jeans pocket and sank into the chair. He took the one next to her.

"Fine." Her breath came out in a huff. "The caffeine will wake me up for when we go look for Josh."

"We will leave and search for Josh." He set his mug on the tree stump that served as an end table and listened to the rain pelting the porch roof. "But it's eleven p.m., and the sun is going to set in about fifty minutes. Trust me, we don't want to be out in the darkness and rain. Sunrise is around four a.m., and we can head out then. If we still don't have cell reception, I'd like to head back to the area where I found you, just in case Skye sends help that way."

"Skye. That's why we stopped at the hotshot camp. I wanted to find my friend."

She stood and walked to the edge of the patio, placing her mug on the railing. She turned to him. "I remembered what you called me, by the way. *Diva Dani*. And you yelled at me."

He flinched. Why was he always the villain? Her look of contempt pierced him harder than an arrow from his longbow.

He ran a hand through his hair. "I'm sorry for the way we treated you. And we never should have let you and Josh go up the mountain alone." Not with a handful of SOR members still roaming around.

She nodded, which he took to be an acknowledgment of his apology. Maybe they could strike up a friendship, or at least she could stop fearing for her life around him.

"Why can't I remember anything? I have no idea what happened once I left your base. Other than something bad happened to Josh. I just don't know what."

He stood and leaned a hip against the porch railing. Progress. She didn't flinch as he moved closer to her. "Would you tell me more about the story you were working on? You seemed pretty convinced that there was a secret compound hidden in the woods. You had some pencil-drawn map too."

He wondered how much Dani knew about recent events. He'd been working when smoke-jumper JoJo Butcher had taken down the SOR camp, literally setting the place on fire. They'd even recovered a sample of the bioweapon the group had been testing. But did the reporter already have the inside scoop, or was she fishing for a story?

She felt around in her pockets and pulled out a crumpled paper. "I—I don't remember this." After she looked at it, she gave it to Grizz. "Did Josh and I find this place?"

Grizz looked at the map. He noted the trail and the area where he'd found her. She must have made it to the area marked by a big X on the crude map. "I think you and Josh stumbled onto something. I heard a gunshot. It wasn't a hunter." Her face paled, more from exhaustion than fear. "Look, why don't you rest some more? You clearly know where my bedroom is, so please go lie down and get some sleep. I'll stay up and keep watch, and I'll pack us a few things so we can leave at sunrise."

If he needed a nap, he could take one on the couch. Wouldn't be the first time he fell asleep stretched out on it.

She shook her head. "No, we need to find Josh. He—"

He put a hand on her arm, and she backed up. "Sorry. I didn't mean to scare you. I—" What could he say to win her trust?

He let out a low growl of frustration.

Well, that wouldn't help make her comfortable. "I promise you, we will go look for Josh. And I'm not going to hurt you. Please get some rest. I think I have some clothes my sister Melanie left when she stayed with me, so you can get cleaned up. You might get more of your memories back once your mind has had some time to relax."

"Yes, sleep might help. But I'm taking this with me." She waved the knife at him and marched into the house.

At least she was a fighter. That, he could work with. He didn't deal with the damsel-in-distress type so well. His last relationship had ended when his girlfriend had decided that Grizz's best friend was better suited for her.

And the betrayal still stung.

Dani headed inside to the bathroom, so he went and rummaged through the back of his closet. In a box, he found some jeans, a short-sleeved T-shirt, and a sweatshirt. His sister liked to visit, but when was the last time she'd been around? They'd used to come visit their grandparents all the time as kids. But now Melanie had two children of her own, and Grizz had thrown himself into his work.

How long had Grizz gone without seeing his family? When he wasn't working wildfire season, the word *hermit* applied to him, but it wasn't like he'd planned to be this way. He laid out the clothes on the bed and moved to his lookout on the front porch.

He was much better on his own. Relationships just complicated things, and he liked his life simple. Predictable, in a way. He could trust himself to get the job done, but when it came to others? That was way too unpredictable for his tastes.

But there was nothing routine or simple about today. Dani was in trouble. Josh was missing. And the bad guys were out there. Grizz could feel it in his bones. Something wasn't right about this situation.

After a while, he headed in and settled on the couch so he could continue to puzzle it out and try to figure out how everything fit together. Had she found evidence that the SOR had a secondary hideout? He'd heard talk that they might have another camp, but nothing had been confirmed.

Grizz sat upright. He must have fallen asleep, and now he wondered what had woken him. Then he heard the sound of someone stumbling around in the bedroom.

Exactly at sunrise, Dani emerged from his bedroom, dressed in an oversized gray University of Alaska sweatshirt. She still had on those stupid white fluffy boots. At least they looked comfortable.

"Thank you for the clothes. They mostly fit, and they aren't caked with mud." Her straight blonde hair hung in waves around her face, and she'd washed the mud out. She looked younger now, even though he knew she had to be around his age—thirty-two. Without all the layers of makeup, her true beauty rang through.

He gave her a mug of coffee and a granola bar. "Sorry, I haven't stocked up at the store recently since I don't spend much time up here in the summer. Hopefully we can make it down the mountain and get some breakfast."

She put the coffee on the kitchen table and squinted, pressing a hand against her forehead.

"Does your head still hurt?" he asked.

"I have a pounding headache. I think it's the light from the window. But I just want to get out there and look for Josh."

"It's still raining, but it's not a total downpour, so we should be able to look for him."

He grabbed the backpack of supplies—water, snacks, and other survival gear. His Sig Sauer sat snug on his hip, under his jacket.

They headed to the ATV, and Dani climbed on behind him. She wrapped her arms around his waist. So much for her earlier cringing with fear at his nearness.

Their nice clean clothes wouldn't last long as the ATV sprayed mud. Grizz navigated the treacherous terrain.

"Wow. Those houses below are amazing." She pointed at the mansions built in an exclusive resort area that spread out below them to the west in a break in the trees.

"A few celebrities and politicians that want to get off the grid for a while have summer houses here."

It took about forty-five minutes to get to the spot where he'd found her. Grizz kept trying his phone, but no luck. The storm must have knocked out the cell towers. He'd have to rely on his team to realize he'd run into trouble and send reinforcements. Except why would they? Most likely his crew would assume his mission had been a success and that he'd headed to his cabin for the night. How long would it be before they sent a search party?

The main road that fed the various trails had been washed out.

He stopped the ATV and grabbed his backpack. "We'll have to go on foot from here. But we need to be careful. There are some dangerous things going on in these woods." She'd stumbled into something big, and he couldn't discount her judgment.

He pointed to the boulder beside a slick wash of mud and debris, then up the mountain. "This is where I found you. You fell from up there."

So far, nothing seemed to jog her memory. She stared with wide eyes, taking it all in but saying nothing.

He led her up the hill, picking an easy path that steered clear of the shifting mud and earth that continued to flow down. Grizz kept an eye out for any signs of danger. Just in case any gunmen from yesterday were still around.

Dani turned in a circle, waving her arms. "This

is so frustrating. Why can't I remember? Nothing looks familiar."

Wet leaves and branches mashed into the earth under his boots. His legs burned with the exertion. Last night's sprint in the mud had taken a toll on him. If he was aching, Dani must be—

"What's that?" Dani picked up her pace.

He followed her pointed finger. Something glinted in the flickering sunlight through the trees.

Grizz hiked to the spot and saw the object half stuck in the earth. He picked it up and wiped the dirt away with the edge of his sleeve. "It's a camera."

He handed it to her.

"It's Josh's camera." Her eyes filled with tears. "He . . . he was taking pictures." She squinted her eyes as if recreating memories of herself and Josh, in those matchy INN windbreakers, taking pictures. Maybe they'd taken pictures of something they shouldn't have. Was that what had happened to her friend?

She took the SIM card out of the camera and shoved it into her pocket to protect it from the rain. "We need to retrieve the images on the SIM card. It might have evidence on it. Can I put the camera in your bag to keep it dry?"

He took the device from her and added it to his backpack.

Grizz patrolled the mountain with his eyes. Someone might be looking for that camera. He crossed his arms. "I don't like this. We need to head down the mountain. We don't know who is out here."

She shook her head so hard her hood slid back. "I have to find Josh. It's the only way I'll get my memories back. We need to keep hiking."

He winced, not liking that he'd lost control of the situation. Since when was she in charge of their survival? But he knew she'd never let it go if he forced her to head to town.

"Fine." It was more of a grunt than a word.

Silence consumed the air around them except for the occasional snap of a twig under their feet.

Grizz jumped in front of her, taking the lead. They weren't on any kind of discernible trail.

"Do you know where we're headed?" she whispered. In the quiet of the mountain, her words reverberated like she'd shouted them at the top of her lungs.

He shook his head and glanced back, waiting for her to catch up. "I'm trying to follow the map and recreate where you walked. Why don't you tell me what you remember now while we hike?

I really want to find Josh fast so we can get out of here. I have a bad feeling about all of this."

She sighed and squinted her eyes, as if that would make the memories from the last twenty-four hours materialize. "I received a tip about a secret bunker or lab of some kind. I know the FBI shut down the SOR base camp, but my source believes there must be another location."

"And they need the help of a reporter to investigate?"

She shrugged. "My source's hands have been tied. They believe the incidents this summer indicate something bigger is at work, like a terrorism plot. But someone high up in the government has quashed any kind of investigation. I'm here to get to the truth."

Terrorism?

Grizz led the way up the mountain, his hopes of finding Josh shredding with each step. If what Dani was telling him was true, Josh didn't stand a chance against these ruthless men.

"What else do you remember about yesterday?" His question was interrupted by a glowing pair of amber eyes peering from the dense area of shrubs. A low growl gave them plenty of warning to take the long way around the bushes.

He touched Dani's shoulder and moved them away from the area. "Coyote," Grizz whispered.

Dani gulped. "Did you bring your longbow?"

He couldn't stifle a chuckle. "I'll handle the coyote. We'll take the long way around for now. And when we get off the mountain and find safety, I'll teach you how to use the longbow."

Just like that, he'd invited Dani one step farther into his life. As if she would be sticking around this place once Josh was found and her world was safe again. What was he thinking?

When they were far removed from the coyote's presence, Dani answered Grizz's prior question. "We stopped at the hotshot camp, where we were turned away by you and a few of your friends."

He ran a hand through his thick, wavy hair and lamented not getting a haircut earlier. "Yeah. We have some bad blood between us and your network. The coverage of a fire from earlier in the summer where a group of homes was lost didn't exactly paint us as heroes."

"But I had nothing to do with that story. I even advocated that they not air it. It was all for the ratings anyway."

A buzzing sound zipped through the air. They froze.

"Wha—"

Grizz covered her mouth with his hand and pulled her behind some trees. He uncovered her mouth but kept both arms around her in a bear hug. She was warm against his chest, and her hair was tickling his cheek, smelling like his shampoo.

There was no electrical grid on this side of the mountain. He let go of her to part the bushes and saw the source of the noise. From their vantage point, they overlooked a small valley enclosed by rock walls on all sides.

A compound had been carved out of the mountain. Complete with electricity and armed guards.

"I guess you were right." Grizz took it all in.

Two men with rifles slung over their shoulders patrolled the edge of the property. One man served as lookout in a stand perched above the main windowless building. A few other structures dotted the compound, but it was the steel-doored factory-looking structure that sent his nerves humming. Whatever was going on in there wasn't good.

"I—I have to get out of here. Something bad happened here. I—Josh—guns . . ."

She wriggled out of his arms and took off down the mountain. He needed to get to her before one of the men discovered their location.

The gunman turned and pointed the scope in the direction of Grizz.

Too late.

Time to run.

THREE

DANI SPRINTED—MORE LIKE SLID—
down the side of the mountain. Probably making
enough racket for the gunmen to pinpoint their
precise location. But she didn't care.

Something bad had happened in these woods,
and she'd seen it with her own eyes.

Everything within her told her to flee. *Now.*

Random images swirled around her but not
enough to create a full picture. The sound of a
gunshot echoed in her mind. Josh. *Shot.*

Instead of reliving that moment, her thoughts
flashed back to his face that Tuesday morning
when she'd followed Josh into the break room and
begged him to go to Alaska with her. She'd been
so sure of herself, confident that this story would

pan out and she'd be back on top of her career. And she couldn't handle the other cameraman that'd jumped at the chance to go on the trip. Ben had asked her out repeatedly, and she had a rule about dating coworkers. She trusted Josh not to hit on her the whole trip.

He'd reluctantly agreed to accompany her. They'd even talked about having some time for sightseeing.

How naïve she'd been.

Grizz caught her elbow. "Slow down, take your time. We need to look out for—"

A bullet exploded into a tree trunk next to them, sending wood chips flying.

"Time to go, princess." Grizz grabbed her arm and raced through the trees.

She struggled to keep up with his punishing pace as he cut through the brush where there was no trail in sight. Apparently, he wanted them to forge their own path—anything to get away from the gunmen. The man knew his way around the trees, zigzagging through the forest.

After they had run at marathon pace in silence for what seemed like an eternity, she slowed, unable to keep up anymore. She heard nothing behind them but was afraid to look. "Do you think we lost them?"

Grizz slowed his pace to match hers. "I don't see them, but that doesn't mean they aren't right behind us. And we've gone in the opposite direction of the ATV. We'll need to backtrack at some point so we can make our way to the cabin. The trail is still washed out. Getting far away from the compound will be the safest option."

"No." She stopped, putting her fists on her hips. "We still need to find Josh."

He glared at her, nostrils flaring. "Are you crazy? Men with guns are chasing us through the woods. I care about finding Josh, but—"

"No buts." She stood strong in the face of his anger, her burning desire to do right by Josh prevailing. "It's my fault that he came out here in the first place. I won't leave him behind."

The tight crinkles around his eyes relaxed. "Fine. I think I know where we are, and there's a cave we can hide in until we know the coast is clear. But we're not equipped to do anything more than defend ourselves against these men. We need to get help, or we'll be overpowered. I have a gun, but we may be outnumbered, and they seem to have some pretty sophisticated firepower."

Dani nodded and trudged next to Grizz. He moved tree branches out of her way while they walked.

"Why is it your fault, Dani? Josh came out here of his own free will. You couldn't have known this would happen."

She huffed out a breath. "He didn't want to come. I convinced him to make the trip from DC because he's one of the few people at work that I trust. I had to get the story."

He guided her by the elbow to change direction. How did he know where they were going? All the trees and rocks looked the same, as if they were walking in circles.

"Tell me more about this story you were working on. You said your boss gave you some sort of ultimatum?"

She flinched. "I said that? Well, I guess it doesn't matter. Everyone knows I'm a failure." She ran her fingers through her blonde hair, shaking a fistful of mud onto the ground.

He waited for her to continue.

She dropped her hands to her sides, fists clenched tight. "Do you remember, around three years ago, hearing about a senator who'd embezzled money in a real-estate scam? I was the reporter who broke the story about Senator Geoff Deville. The story went national after he bilked a lot of people out of money in the investment scheme. There was a trial, and he was acquitted, but not before the public ridiculed him and his wife left him. He was found innocent, and apparently someone else was behind the whole thing. He came off looking like a victim, and my story became a complete work of fiction."

She huffed out a long breath. "The public turned on me. I became the laughingstock of journalism, and the senator became a victim of sloppy reporting. This lead in Alaska was . . . *is* my way to stay in the public's good graces. I can't fail. I won't fail. Second place is still losing. My boss told me not to come home without a story, so that's what I'll do."

Her resolve began to crumble. Here she was, covered from head to toe in mud, revealing her biggest regret.

And Grizz remained silent. Because he agreed with those people who had messaged her on social media and told her she should quit? Or with the guy at the store who'd cornered her in produce and told her she was the worst kind of person?

She'd shared her story with him. Now it was his turn. "So, Grizz, what's your deal? I'm sure there's a reason you're living in the woods by yourself. What's your story?"

He stomped on.

She stepped in front of him and faced him.

"I'm a reporter, you know. I can see you've got secrets, and I'm the best there is at getting people to talk."

More growling. "Less talking, more walking."

"Ah. So there's something to talk about."

He marched around her. "Sure. I live at the Midnight Sun base camp all summer long. End of story."

She followed him, certain that was *not* the end of it—or the beginning. "Please, tell me what happened. It might make me trust you more. Because the jury's still out on if you're a good guy or a total creep who just happens to be keeping me alive. You yelled at me when we first met. I've never been talked down to by anyone like that. What gives?"

"I didn't yell." His voice echoed and he winced. He lowered his tone. "Okay, I may have raised my voice. But you came to the wrong camp to ask for help. Why would you want a 'lukewarm shot' to help you anyway?"

And there it was.

That horrible moniker her station had splashed across every screen in the country after a wildfire had burned too close to some expensive homes. "Why do you have to be such a brute? I had nothing to do with that story and the name. I told my producers it was a terrible idea."

He reached for her elbow, but she folded her arms. "I believe we've already had this conversation."

He shot her a look. "How noble of you to defend us lowly backcountry hicks. But you have no idea what hotshots do. You live in your DC high-rise with no clue how to survive in the real world. You shouldn't have been poking around the Alaskan mountains looking for trouble."

Dani shot him a look right back in his smug face. "I'm not as ditzy as you make me out to be. Skye's my friend, remember? I've heard her stories about smokejumpers. I even thought it would make a nice news piece one day. But are we really going to have this argument in the middle of the forest with gunmen on our tail, Mr. Hotshot? If I hadn't come here, you guys might have never found the compound. Now the authorities will take the threat seriously."

He stopped and she turned to face him.

"Don't worry. I don't need you to save me. I can take care of myself."

"Like I said before, nothing is stopping you." He waved his arms as if to usher her forward.

Dani pivoted and stormed off in the opposite

direction, just to prove her point. The man was infuriating. Sure, she liked to be clean, tucked into her warm bed, not traipsing around the mud and—

Grizz tackled her like a linebacker and took her to the ground. A bullet whizzed by the place she'd just stood. Her face hit the dirt, and his weight on her knocked the air from her lungs. He rolled off her, grabbed her arm, and had them running in the span of half a second.

Oh no. It turned out she actually did need this man.

Being wrong was the *worst*.

Every time he opened his mouth, he proved Dani right.

He'd vowed he'd be nice from now on, but she'd dug her heels in and turned all reporter on him. And that poked the bear in him.

Why do you have to be such a brute? Her question gnawed at his twisted insides.

He didn't owe her answers—he just needed to get them off the mountain. Alive. Then he'd be rid of the reporter, and the authorities could raid that compound. It wasn't his job to get involved any more than handing the information over to the FBI.

There! A rock formation with a hollowed-out section at the base. He dropped to the ground and slid through the opening.

He pulled Dani by the arm, and they ducked into the crevice between the rocks. There was barely enough room for his six-foot-two frame, but he managed to tuck her in next to him. Hopefully the gunmen would be looking up and miss the opening.

"Are we safe?" Dani whispered, her face close to his.

His arms were wrapped around her, and her hair tickled his nose.

Crunching sounds stopped his reply before the words could form. Through the fissure in the rocks, he saw Army-issued black boots topped with cargo pants.

"Do you see them?" a voice called out.

"Negative."

"Let's get to the compound and make sure they didn't double back."

The steps retreated, but he still held his breath, afraid to move. Dani trembled and made a squeak. Her whole body went rigid.

Please, please, Dani. Don't make a sound.

What had her spooked—

Something brushed against his leg, and he instinctively tried to kick it away in the small confines. The animal hissed.

Not good.

"What is that thing?" Dani whispered.

"It may be a rat or marmot. We just need to stay perfectly still. They don't bite." Maybe. He'd made that last part up because he had no idea, but he didn't want to stress her out any more. Marmots could be violent when it came to protecting their turf.

Whatever it was, the animal circled their feet and chirped. Dani hiccupped a squeal. She was squished against Grizz to the point that he couldn't tell if it was his thumping heartbeat or hers.

"I can't take this much more. I'm not good in tight spaces with rats." Dani shifted but then settled down.

They held steady for what seemed like an eternity but was probably only ten minutes. Unless it was a ruse to get them to come out, the men had retreated.

"I think it's safe to climb out." He let go of his hold on her, more reluctant to do that than he was okay with. As if she'd welcome his touch when they weren't in mortal danger.

She shimmied out of the cave opening first, and Grizz followed. He looked into the hole they'd just crawled out of and saw the ticked-off marmot.

"We got a little too close to her babies." Grizz pointed at the nest of baby marmots. "No wonder she kept moving around."

Dani shuddered. "That was as close as I ever want to be to wildlife."

Grizz looked around for signs of the men or danger. This wasn't over. Those guys might return with reinforcements from the compound. After all, this was twice now that someone had found their camp.

Had they found his ATV yet?

"We still can head to the ATV. If they went back to camp, they might not have spotted it yet."

Dani nodded, a shell-shocked look in her eyes. "Yes, let's get out of here. You're right, we need to get help. These men are dangerous, and whatever they've done to Josh, they could do to us."

"If only I had a recording to replay your words. *You're right.*"

She elbowed him and he pretended it hurt. "You've only saved my life three times now. I'll admit that I'm out of my element, but don't count me out just yet."

That was one thing he'd never do again. Underestimate Dani Barlowe. The woman was tenacious in her quest for the truth. He loved that fighting spirit in her. While she might not have his survival skills in the wilds of Alaska, she could hold her own.

He guided them to the area where he'd stashed the ATV, using the sun as an indicator of their direction.

"How do you know how to navigate so well?"

"I was born and raised in Alaska. Grew up in Copper Mountain, not too far from where we are. My cousin has a summer home out here, and we spent a lot of time there with my family." Well, before he'd disappointed them all. Now that his father had passed, he rarely saw his mom or sister anymore.

"It's really beautiful out here. And peaceful."

Had he really experienced peace on this mountain? It was more of a refuge for him to keep the storms at bay. He'd worked too hard to keep people out to let peace in. His judgment was flawed when it came to trusting people, so it was easier to just keep people at a distance.

But somehow, Dani had snuck through his security perimeter.

She kept talking, chattering like a bird in spring. "It makes me think of God, in a way. I don't actually believe in a God who cares about our mundane lives. I mean, my mom always made my sister and me go to church every Sunday. But it's different when you think about the fact that someone had to create all of this." She gestured to the thick trees all around them.

"You don't believe God cares?" Hmm. That kind of sounded like him. His grandfather had been the most faithful man on the planet, but Grizz just couldn't trust that easily. Not when God hadn't saved his friend's life.

She shrugged, her sweatshirt crusted with mud. But it didn't matter what she wore; the woman still looked like she'd spent hours putting together her outfit.

And why was he looking at her in that way?

"As far as I've seen, it's more like God is mean."

"Really?" He pushed a branch out of her way. "Most of the church services I attended as a kid said the opposite. That God loves us. Unconditionally." Even if that hadn't been his experience.

"No one loves unconditionally. Eventually

we'll fail—we fail each other, and someone always gets hurt. And then we're on our own."

"I kind of agree with you." He'd rather take action now than trust a God he couldn't see. At least he'd be doing something rather than waiting around for a God who might show up. Or not.

She stopped short. "No way. Something we have in common finally?"

"I just think God is too capricious to trust Him with what I love. I prefer to take care of things myself."

"And if you can't?"

Well, that was when he'd become a hermit—when he wasn't with the hotshot crew—and shut everyone out of his personal life rather than let them down. Again. But he wasn't ready to say that to Dani.

The reporter was shaking him down for a story, and he refused to be her next headline.

Grizz stopped short and sniffed.

"What is it?" Dani's eyes darted around.

"A storm is coming. I can smell it." To prove his point, thunder rumbled in the distance, and the clouds swirled overhead. A breeze rustled through the tree branches.

But there was a different smell that had Grizz concerned.

The smell of death.

Buzzards circled in the distance. The ATV was still about a quarter mile away, and those birds spelled trouble. They'd have to walk by them.

It could be a dead animal, but Grizz's gut twisted in an unrelenting knot.

Up ahead lay a mound of dirt. The kind that signaled a shallow grave. And then Grizz saw it. A sneaker sticking out of the heap of earth.

"Hey, Dani?" He needed to guide her gently through this.

Dani pulled up short. "Oh no. No. No."

Oh no was an understatement.

"It can't be. That's Josh's sneaker. I used to make fun of how much he spent on those designer Nikes." Dani rushed to the spot. Her hand flew to cover her face. She tripped a few feet in front of the mound and sobbed.

Grizz got on the ground next to Dani and crushed her against his chest. "Don't look, Dani. Just don't look."

Grizz used a tree branch to brush away some of the dirt to uncover a man's lifeless face.

They'd found Josh, and a bullet hole in the man's temple revealed the dangerous game these militiamen were playing.

He had to get Dani out of the woods. These men were full-blown killers.

FOUR

SHE'D KILLED JOSH WHITLOCK.

Even if someone else had pulled the trigger, this was all her fault, and Dani knew it.

Fierce tears burned down her cheeks. She wiped her face on Grizz's shirt and wiggled out of his arms. His body was warm and safe in a way she hadn't expected. Not when they'd just been talking about how she couldn't rely on anyone—even God. Would Grizz be any different? She couldn't expect him to come to her rescue all the time.

Except the man stepped up every time she was in danger. Here he was, trying to shield her from Josh's body.

She shivered and made sure to keep her back

to Josh, but she'd already seen too much. The imprint of Josh's twisted body and lifeless eyes were seared permanently in her brain.

"It's all my fault. I was so determined to track down the story. He didn't want to come with me, but the station offered him overtime. I ruined another life, just like with the senator. I did this." The memories still hung out of reach. Why couldn't she remember what had happened once they'd left the hotshot camp? But it didn't matter. "I was the reason he was in the woods. His death is on me."

Grizz let go of her to move her away from the gruesome scene. "It's not your fault. Evil exists in this world. What happened to your friend was a result of criminals hiding in the woods. You had no idea what you were walking into."

He held her and let her cry.

"Please help me tell Josh's story. We need to see these men brought to justice. I don't want Josh's death to be in vain. Something good has to come from it."

Grizz's arms tightened around her. "First we need to get to shelter. This storm is going to intensify, and we don't want to get caught in another mudslide. Let's find the ATV and head to my cabin. It's too treacherous to get to the other roads leading off the mountain, and the main access is cut off with the mudslide. We can try once the rain lets up, but I'm worried about more roads being washed away before the storm lets up. It's too risky. But we won't let these men get away with this."

More tears fell, and she wiped them with the back of her mud-covered wrist.

He let her go but gripped her hand.

Dani walked with him, finding solace in his strong fingers wrapped around hers. Finally, they came to the clearing with the ATV. The ride to the cabin felt like an eternity, while in reality it was probably thirty minutes. The roller coaster of emotions had her wanting to scream, hit something, do anything to release the pressure building inside of her.

She'd led Josh straight to his death. It should have been her, not him.

Grizz pulled up to the cabin just as a crack of thunder rumbled. Dani shivered, her wet clothes sticking to her. Grizz opened the front door.

"I—can I—" Words fell off her tongue.

He nodded. "Why don't you use the bathroom and take a hot shower?"

She added *mind reader* to her mental list of

Grizz's talents, right next to bow hunter and marmot wrangler.

"I'll make us something to eat. You can also take my bedroom again. I washed your clothes last night while you slept, and they're on the dresser."

Why had she stormed off earlier? Like she could survive a minute without this man. Now he was playing host to her, making sure she had everything she needed. "Thank you."

She wanted to clean up, but the draw of Grizz and his steady strength had her hanging back. Watching him move around his house. His *home*.

He busied himself in the kitchenette, pulling out pots and ingredients from his sparse cabinets. "I just want to make sure you're safe. I never should have sent you off on your own like that."

"You didn't know what would happen to Josh and me. But thanks for showing up and saving my life. More than once. And protecting me from . . . you know . . . marmots and everything else."

Grizz glanced over his shoulder, a soft smile on his face.

Dani watched the man in the kitchen. His bulky frame seemed out of place in the tiny area. "You like to cook?"

He turned around. "I guess. I have a freezer, and I love to grill in the summertime."

She never would have expected a man like Grizz knew his way around a kitchen. But his soup was fantastic.

Dani heeded his advice and showered. The hot water washed away the dirt and mud but did nothing to scrub away the images of finding Josh dead in the woods.

After the shower, she headed to the bedroom. Her original clothes were folded neatly on the dresser. For a rough-looking guy, he kept a neat house. Cooked. Did laundry.

She sank onto the bed, which had a cozy comforter for a bachelor's reclusive cabin in the woods. Something she hadn't noticed before— because she hadn't been willing to *see* it. Smells from the kitchen called to her.

Grizz had a Bible on his nightstand. Why did he have this? She picked it up. The pages were worn, and she noted the name on the cover. *Matthew Grizz.*

Was this Grizz's first name? She flipped through a few more pages and determined that Matthew must be Grizz's grandfather, since this used to be his family's cabin.

Too bad. She really wanted to solve the mystery of Grizz's first name. But she had learned that Grizz was surprisingly sentimental. After all, he'd saved his grandfather's Bible.

She opened the old book with yellowing pages, and it fell open to a z called Philippians. She read the highlighted verse.

I can do all things through Christ who strengthens me.

She sighed. "Except keep my friend alive."

She tossed the book onto the bed.

All things?

If life had taught her anything, it was that it was up to Dani to make things happen. That was what made her a successful reporter.

Win at all costs. Wasn't that the mantra her dad had drilled into her head growing up?

Now she was out here alone, with no way to call her parents and tell them she was still alive. Fatigue weighed her down. When was the last time she'd called them, or even had lunch with her friends?

She had to get out of this funk. Talking to Grizz might lighten up her dark thoughts about God, death, and the dead body that haunted her mind. But it was hardly going to solve any of her problems.

Yet she found herself drawn to the big muscle man.

She headed out the front door to the porch. The rhythmic sound of the beating raindrops soothed her soul, even if the peace didn't last. It never did. But being out in the woods, so remote, with no cell phone or internet, she found herself not missing those things.

She looked out beyond the railing. Trees rose up a hill in the distance, but the clouds hung low, creating a fog. The sun still shone brightly for five in the afternoon. She wore another one of Grizz's sister's hoodie sweatshirts that had the University of Alaska emblem across the front. Her own jacket hadn't survived.

When was the last time she'd felt this alive? At home, it was go go go. She never stopped to take in the scenery. Alaska was bringing out a different side of her—one that she hadn't known she possessed. Here, she didn't have to be driven to perform.

She could just . . . rest.

Grizz stepped outside with plates and cups in hand. "I made us some lunch." He motioned to another tree-stump end table, where he set two full mugs of coffee. "I poured you some coffee.

Hope you like venison. I've got a ton of deer meat in my freezer."

"I don't think I've ever had venison."

The rain had a sweet aroma, but it was another scent that sparked her interest. What was it? Aftershave?

"Thanks for everything, especially the coffee. I've got to maintain my perky disposition somehow." She slid into the rocker next to Grizz and tried not to check him out in his tight T-shirt and jeans. How did he find clothes in his size?

"Yeah, it must be hard being on camera all the time. I'd never make it as a reporter."

She took a bite of the delicious stew. The flavors melted in her mouth. "This stew is amazing."

She snuck a glance at him. The man knew how to clean up, she realized. Another thing she was only just noticing. His beard was neatly trimmed, and she was growing more accustomed to his mountain-man vibe.

"What are we going to do about Josh?"

Grizz sat back in his chair.

She stared out over the landscape. "Are we safe here? Will those men find us?"

Grizz looked at her. "I have some security features that warn me if anyone gets too close to my property. So far, everything is quiet."

She wrapped her palms around the warm mug, relishing the peace of the Alaskan mountains. "I saw your Bible on the shelf in your room. I thought you weren't exactly the believing kind of man."

He shrugged. "It was my grandfather's. I kept it more for the memory of him, sitting in this chair every morning with a pen, marking up the pages. But I read it occasionally."

He offered her a plaid fleece throw blanket, and she wrapped herself up in a cocoon.

"Do you actually believe that you can do anything with God's help?"

Grizz looked at her, his dark-green eyes reflecting a depth of sorrow she hadn't noticed before.

Then he looked away from her and rocked in his chair. "God and I aren't on the best terms. I grew up going to church, but I'm not sure God is going to intervene when I need Him to. Or at least, He hasn't yet."

Hmm. Maybe she and the mountain man had more in common than she'd thought.

She sipped her coffee. "I grew up always having to make a way for myself. If I didn't do it, no one else would. My father was my gymnastics coach when I was twelve, and we were heading to the Olympics. Second place wasn't an option. I still hear his voice ringing through my ears. 'Second place is last place. You still lost.' So next time, I'd work twice as hard. Until an injury took me out of the competition for good."

"Wow. That's a lot for a young teenager to deal with. I can see why that makes you work twice as hard to track down your leads. It made you a great reporter. But at what cost?"

Exactly her sentiment. "It cost me time. Time with family, friends, building relationships. It's lonely always having to work for that number-one spot. And then maintain it. There's always someone younger and more skilled coming right up behind you. It's exhausting."

She closed her eyes, relishing the quiet Alaskan air, allowing the memories to flow. "My dad eventually left my mom, and I rarely speak to him. Yet I'm still trying to live up to his expectations."

Grizz cleared his throat, obviously not used to dealing with emotions—his or other people's. "We need to look at that SIM card. I didn't push you earlier because I wanted to give you time to grieve the loss of your friend, but tell me more about your source. You said you trusted the person?"

She opened her eyes and burrowed deeper into the blanket. "I do trust them." He probably knew Rio, since Grizz worked with Skye, but Dani had always kept confidentiality sacred and wasn't about to reveal who had brought her here.

A memory hit her like a bolt of lightning. "There's a building with a smokestack and white smoke puffing out of it. I—I must have seen their lab in the woods at that compound. There were armed men dragging someone into it. That has to be the location."

Grizz nodded. "I saw that building in the middle of the compound. It stood out from the rest of them. Do you have the SIM card?"

"I left it on the nightstand. I'll get it if you have a computer. Hopefully, seeing the images will jog my memories. Because I want to get to the bottom of what happened on that mountain."

Grizz dug under his kitchen cabinet for his laptop, trying to shake the image of a sobbing Dani from his mind. The woman had been put through the wringer.

Would looking at these pictures help or hurt?

And when had Dani blown through the security checkpoint that guarded his heart? It scared him how much he cared.

But he'd do anything to take this pain away from her.

He set up the laptop on his kitchen table, and Dani returned with the SIM card. She dug the camera out of the backpack. "Do you have a USB cable? We can read the chip off the camera."

"Maybe." He dug around in the cabinet and pulled out a spider web of tangled cords. One of these had to be the right one.

She stood with her hands on her hips. "Just give me whatever cables you have."

She huffed and muttered something under her breath to the effect of "At least you're good-looking."

Had he heard her correctly?

He mentally filed that comment away for later.

She pulled out a cable for the laptop and plugged it in while wiping six layers of dust off the machine with her sweatshirt sleeve. "This computer belongs in a museum. I'm not even sure it will turn on." She continued to untangle the cords. "Bingo." She pulled a thin black cable out of the pile. "This is what we need to connect the camera. Assuming this dinosaur cooperates."

He dished out more venison stew into their bowls and brought them over, sliding into a seat across the corner from her. She downed her second bowl.

She hit the power button, and the laptop chugged to life. Dani eyed him. "Why are you living like a hermit in the woods? No Wi-Fi. No television. Ancient technology. Why?"

She *had* to go there. He shrugged. "There's no story here, Dani. It's just my life. Sorry it doesn't live up to your high standards." He checked his phone. Still no cell signal. All he had was his closed-circuit cameras and security system that weren't online.

She cocked her head. "Do I look like I give up that easily?"

If only she looked a little deeper, she'd realize there was more to Grizz than some loner living in the woods. How would she feel about him if she found out the truth? His friend Kyle had died because Grizz had trusted the wrong person.

He bit back a growl. "Just get that camera working."

Boy, this reporter went after stories with no signs of backing down. Nothing was off-limits as far as she was concerned. The woman had a way of taking the most innocent situations and turning them into a therapy session. She seemed sure she'd find a way to get him to talk.

But Grizz wasn't going to let her crack him, even if his admiration for her had inched up a few notches. She had zero wilderness survival skills, but she had a brand of fierceness that he couldn't match, even if he had survived basic training in the Army.

At least she wasn't afraid of him at the moment.

The screen lit up, and so did Dani's face. "Well, we don't have internet on this relic, but at least we have a screen. Let me see if I can get the card to connect." She fiddled with the wires and laptop. "It looks like Josh has some videos on the camera too. Let's look at the pictures. Hopefully, the images will jog my memories."

Grizz moved to the table to look at the screen, but he stopped short of touching her shoulder. "You don't have to do this if you don't want. We don't know what's in these pictures. I can look at them to make sure they aren't too . . . intense."

Dani's eyes widened. "I appreciate the concern. But I have to know what I saw that night. I'm prepared for the consequences of seeing the truth."

She couldn't shoot a longbow, but the woman could stare death in the face and not flinch.

The laptop dinged and Dani clicked a few times. A square with an image popped up.

Grizz leaned over Dani far enough to smell a rather masculine-scented shampoo. His shampoo. Of course, he had nothing froufrou for her to use. But he didn't hate the smell on her.

Josh had taken photos and videos. Dani opened the first video, which gave a bird's-eye view of the area. Grizz figured they had to have been up on the ridge looking down on the area.

She brought up the next video, which zoomed in on the building with the smokestack.

"It's just like I remembered," Dani whispered. "The white smoke pouring out of the chimney."

The video continued, and they watched an older man being dragged through the compound, flanked by two men. The camera shot got a close-up of faces.

One man had a tattoo across his neck. Dani paused the video, and Grizz sucked in a breath. The man in the still frame wore a scowl and had a gun trained on the hostage's temple. Grizz knew he'd seen the gunman before. But where?

He racked his brain. The FBI notice. "He's bad news, Dani. I remember now. Rio Parker sent out an alert. I think his name is Jeremiah Redding. He's on the FBI's Most Wanted list. He managed to escape when everything went down at the SOR base camp, so Rio sent out his description, including that snake tattoo."

Dani wasn't listening. She pointed at the screen to the man standing behind Redding. "It can't be. How?"

"That man looks a lot like—"

"Senator Geoff Deville. But why would he be in the compound in the woods?" There was no mistaking the tall man's silver hair that stood out in the black-and-white footage. Not to mention Josh had zoomed in on his face.

"Could the senator be involved? I mean, this group is well-funded and well-connected. I still don't understand how they've stayed hidden for so long."

If the senator was involved, they were sitting on a gold mine of evidence the FBI would want. This could take down a dirty politician. But the reality of their find meant Grizz had to get Dani and the evidence off this mountain. If these men knew the camera footage existed, they'd be on Grizz's front doorstep in a second.

Dani was the lynchpin to taking down this entire operation.

Tears dripped down Dani's cheek. "I—I remember. I had the camera rolling. When they shot Josh."

He pulled a chair up next to her and held her hand. "Don't watch it, Dani. You did a great job getting this evidence. I'm going to make sure this gets to the authorities."

He closed the laptop screen with the hand that wasn't clutching hers. She didn't need to see any more.

"Josh's death isn't on you, Dani. I know what it's like to lose someone and feel the burden of failure. It's not your fault. Sometimes things are out of your control."

"I don't deal well with being out of control. It's why I work so hard to control the things I can." She stood, renewed determination flashing in her eyes. "How are we going to expose the truth? We need to get this evidence to the authorities. For Josh."

He checked his phone for the hundredth time. Still no signal. What was happening on the mountain that had knocked out all communications?

The storms? Or these men in the compound?

"We'll get these guys. But whatever happens, we're in this together. Don't go rogue on me now, Dani."

A snapping sound stopped his heart. Even though he was low tech, he had plenty of security features built around his cabin. And someone had just set off one of his booby traps.

He put a finger up to his lips. "We're not alone," he whispered.

In order to save her and get her evidence to town, Grizz would have to show Dani a side of himself he never showed anyone.

"Time to make our way to the outhouse."

FIVE

DANI'S ENTIRE BODY WENT RIGID, and she refused to move even a millimeter until Grizz gave her the all clear.

Grizz raced to the front window, his eyes patrolling his property. Dani sat at the kitchen table and tried to summon her bravery. She was not meant for this kind of life off the grid.

She hadn't told her family or friends where she was headed before she'd jumped on the first flight to Alaska. She kept patting her pockets as if her phone would magically reappear. If she hadn't lost her phone, she could have at least checked in with her mom and sister.

"What is it?" she whispered. Was he going to start joking about outhouses again?

If he was concerned, she was downright frightened. Nothing seemed to rattle this guy.

He didn't respond immediately but continued his search out the window, his body language on high alert. Without taking his eyes off the window, he answered with his voice low. "Someone set off my first perimeter alert."

He had more than one? The low-tech mountain man had earned himself a few points with his homemade security system. He wasn't letting anything near his cabin.

"Human or animal?" Dani prayed for a bear, a coyote, or anything other than the ruthless men that had murdered Josh.

He sucked in a breath and rushed toward the kitchen. "Human. Stay where you are and away from the window. I saw a flash of camo in the woods. They've found us."

"What are we going to do?" Dani tried to keep her voice even, but it came out super shrill. She shoved the SIM card in her pocket for safekeeping. "We're sitting ducks in this small cabin. There's nowhere to hide. And what are you doing?"

He ignored her and shoved the refrigerator away from the wall.

"We both can't fit behind the refrigerator,

not to mention we'd be trapped." She stood and moved to investigate.

He grappled with the ancient appliance. "If you'd stop talking and just trust me for a second . . . I might not be a computer genius, but I've got plenty of tricks up my sleeve."

He rolled the refrigerator out of its place and crouched to pull at the floor panel. A square lifted to reveal stairs below.

Dani blinked. "A secret passage?"

He stepped into the opening, the wooden stairs groaning under his weight.

"Come on." He motioned her forward, and she took the first steps into the dark hole. He helped her to the bottom and pulled the chain on a light.

Grizz moved up the stairs and pulled a string that rolled the refrigerator back—she now noticed it was on a track—and it reset right into place.

Dani spun around to take in her surroundings. "You have an underground bunker. Oh, wow." Along one wall of the square room, racks of cases held every kind of weapon imaginable, all under locked glass panels.

She heard Grizz descend the steps.

"Another longbow?" She pointed at what

looked like a weapon straight out of a fantasy movie.

"Yes, but I'm more interested in the guns right now. I only saw one man creeping around outside, but that doesn't mean there won't be more."

Her mind spun, creating an amazing news feature. *Life Off the Grid.* Too bad this mountain man would never sit for an interview. Because this underground bunker was a gold mine of story ideas. Grizz had a lair!

"How long can we survive down here?"

"Weeks, probably. Not that we'll want to stay holed up that long." He shrugged and unlocked a wall cabinet filled with gallons of water, military meal kits, and row after row of canned preserves. He even had a fuel source, not to mention a portable grill and coffee pot. A freezer hummed on one side of the ten-by-ten room. How had he gotten that down the stairs? That must be where he kept the venison.

"You canned these things?"

"The berries grow wild, and there are way too many to eat." He frowned. "A man can't cook and can things?" He harrumphed for emphasis, and she let out a laugh, then slapped a hand across her mouth.

When was the last time she'd laughed out loud,

spontaneous and free? Now was not the time to give into the urge.

Grizz went to one wall and pulled a panel aside. She had to get the man talking. This doomsday prepper had a story to tell. "How did you know the first perimeter was breached? Do you have booby traps set up? Tell me everything. I feel like we're sitting ducks down here."

He grabbed a backpack and started filling it with food and water. "I set a series of alerts that let me know if someone is prowling around. I have a motion sensor, high enough so an animal won't set it off. But it sends an alert to my phone through my closed-circuit connection. Which is great, since the cellular service is down."

"And there's a second perimeter?" She watched him move to a safe, open it, and add two guns and some ammo to the bag.

"Honey, there are four perimeters." Amusement flashed in his eyes.

She tried to hide her interest—and her reaction to his calling her "honey"—but her eyes involuntarily widened. "How will we know if the second perimeter is breached?"

A chirping sound startled her. Sounded like one of those personal self-defense alarms.

"That's the second perimeter. Time to pack up and move."

He unlocked another cabinet and outfitted himself with knives and a vest—bulletproof, maybe. She patted her pocket where she'd secured the pocketknife he'd given her.

Her fear of Grizz had been replaced by awe. This hotshot, protector, and mystery man with those broad shoulders and strong biceps was going to put his life on the line to save her. Knowing that added to her growing attraction to him.

Admiration. She corrected herself.

It wasn't an attraction.

To prove it, she said, "Grizz, you're the hero in this story all the way around."

He grunted and got back to work. "Yeah, well, from this point forward, you are sworn to secrecy. No stories, nothing made public. Because you are about to see my outhouse."

"I take it you're not taking me to an outdoor bathroom with no plumbing?"

"Just wait."

Another siren chimed from his phone. "Perimeter three?"

He nodded. "They're close to the cabin. Let's go."

"To the outhouse?"

Grizz approached a wall and pushed it.

Dani couldn't hide her delight. "A hidden door. You do have a lot of tricks up your sleeve, No-First-Name Grizz."

He passed her a flashlight, and she illuminated a tunnel, carved out from the rocks.

Great. More tight spaces. "Are there spiders?" The question came out of her mouth before she could filter it. How girlie could she be?

"Nah, no spiders. Just watch out for assassin bugs. Those things hurt."

"Assassin . . ." Did she really want to know more? If only she could get the baby marmots back.

"Just lead the way, Grizz."

He squeezed her hand and didn't let go as he led her into a tunnel. She kept the light trained on the dirt path carved through the mountainside.

Her nerves jangled. "How much weight is above us? You carved a tunnel through the mountain? Could this thing collapse? How far until we get—"

"Do you always ask this many questions?" He chuckled.

At least she wasn't annoying him. "My dad always told me that no one would ever kidnap me.

At least, not for long. I'd talk their ear off because when I get nervous, I get gabby."

She could stand in the tunnel, but Grizz had to duck in spots.

"This takes us to the outhouse. It's a sort of garage I built into the side of the mountain. They'll target the cabin, but we should be safe."

"If we make it to this garage, will you send up your smoke signal from there?"

He chuckled. "I'll try. But the outhouse has a lookout perch. I can see for miles on a clear day, and hopefully the rain will subside enough for me to stop these guys with a long-range rifle."

They trudged on in the near darkness, only the flashlight shining in front of them. Grizz never let go of her. She scanned the area for any creepy-crawlies and willed herself not to scream if she saw an assassin bug. Whatever that might be. She envisioned a giant beetle with knives for legs.

Grizz was the first to reach a set of stairs with a trapdoor at the top. He helped her up and opened the door, folding the hatch over before he climbed out.

She emerged into a massive room. "Oh."

It resembled a steel cave. The floor was concrete, but the walls were reinforced by corrugated metal. The room was built into the side of the mountain. The ceiling consisted of granite and formed a dome at the top. One side of the room held a wooden staircase with a landing that led to a loft area. Where one lone door stood.

The outhouse door.

"Well, this is the first time I've heard you speechless."

She turned to him. He looked proud of his lair. Her heart warmed that he'd shared this with her.

"Over here is where I keep my vehicles." One side of the room served as a garage, with two more ATVs, a dirt bike, a snowmobile, and a dark-green Jeep. All of the toys gleamed from the fluorescent lights running across the roof of the building. The opposite side contained a small kitchen area with a two-burner stove and minifridge.

"Wait. Is there a bathroom? If the outhouse isn't real . . ."

Grizz pointed to the far corner of the area. "There's a modern bathroom complete with running water."

"So you don't hang out in your cabin much," Dani said. "I can see you chilling out back here, watching the sun set from your outhouse loft."

He grinned. "I like it here."

"I . . . I just never imagined"—she waved her arms around the space—"this man cave. I mean, you've got every toy imaginable. Now I get why you like this place so much." She eyed a wall of monitors and put her fists on her hips. "Hey, I thought you didn't have internet or anything high tech. What's this?"

He shook his head. "It's all closed-circuit. I can watch the property, but no one can hack into it. There. Look." He pointed to one of the four monitors.

A man in camo flashed across the screen, a gun slung across his shoulder. Moving fast. Determined to catch them.

Grizz sighed. "I'm sure this guy brought plenty of backup."

A buzz zipped through the air like a crack of thunder.

Dani jumped. "What—"

"The fourth perimeter trap. They're at the cabin."

Dani eyed the ATV. On the far wall, the outline of a garage door was visible. "We should go out the back, make a run for it. They think we're in the house. We need to get the SIM card to the authorities, right?"

"Or"—Grizz picked up one of the bags he'd packed with weapons from the cellar—"we defend this homestead and maybe get out of here alive."

Dani bit her lip.

For the first time since getting lost in the Alaskan wild, she finally saw a way out of her situation. But was Grizz on board?

Running wasn't an option as far as Grizz was concerned. Ever. She didn't understand because, as she'd told him, Dani considered him to be a hero.

Little did she know . . .

He certainly wasn't one, but when his back was up against a wall, he came out fighting.

Grizz mentally kicked himself for not having given that trip wire a higher voltage. The thought of these murderers lurking around this land made his blood boil. If they died, justice for Josh would never come down on them. These guys would get away with everything.

Maybe even something far more serious than one man's death.

Dani explored his garage, probably plotting her escape. The woman was always on the run—acting first and thinking things through second.

He was the complete opposite. All actions were carefully orchestrated.

But as he watched her, he realized her movements were nervous. Would she leave him behind if given the opportunity? He needed to give her a job to do, or she'd drive him crazy with all her relentless questions and chattering.

"I built a lookout at the top." He pointed to a ladder near the front door. "I'm heading up to take a look."

Her dazed expression showed the toll the past twenty-four hours had taken on her. "Lookout? Can't we just make a run for it? We've got the vehicles."

She waved at the garage-style door on the opposite side of the cave. He'd obscured the outside with foliage so that it blended into the side of the cliff, but no one would miss rumbling and groaning as it opened.

"We've also got the firepower," Grizz said. "And since we'll be able to see them before they see us, we have the advantage. You need to trust me. But I could use your help. Another pair of eyes watching for these men would be helpful."

"You—you want me to back you up?" Her eyes flashed with . . . what was that? Pride? Excitement?

So, the key to Dani was not to sideline her. She wanted to be involved in the action. Made sense for a reporter, so he mentally filed the information.

He checked the closed-circuit camera monitors and watched for movement. A man in camo popped in and out of the frame, too fast to get an identity. How many men were they up against?

With his high-power rifle slung across his back, Grizz climbed the stairs to the outhouse door. Dani followed.

Grizz had kept the original outhouse door, but it now served as a decoy. Instead of an old-school bathroom, it led to his outdoor wood loft. The door could be seen from the outside, but the loft was well concealed by the tree line. The six-by-ten platform gave Grizz a view of most of his property, and he could see for miles. Sometimes he'd just hang out in his perch and watch wildlife.

Dani gasped. "This view is amazing. And you have more rocking chairs." She pulled the hood up on her sweatshirt and leaned against the railing.

At nine thirty p.m., the clouds parted momentarily for the sun to show off its glory by throwing hues of yellow, orange, and red across the horizon. The trees looked like they were on fire with the twinkling lights and shifting shadows. Clouds hung low, clinging to the mountainside like cotton candy. A lightning bolt lit up the sky in the distance. More storms were on their way.

"Is it safe to talk?" she whispered.

"As long as we keep our voices low."

"I can't believe you have more rocking chairs. They're magnificently crafted."

Grizz set up his rifle on the railing to look through the scope. "My grandfather built them." He handed her a pair of binoculars. "You cover left, and I'll cover right."

"You really had a special relationship with him."

Grizz nodded. "My father and I never saw eye to eye on things. But spending time in this cabin was the highlight of every summer. If my grandfather were here, he'd tell us to stop and pray. To cast all our cares on the Lord. I can still hear him humming 'Amazing Grace' as he worked on those rocking chairs."

The last time Grizz had prayed was when his grandfather had been dying of cancer. Prayers hadn't changed the situation one bit.

The words flowed through his mind, and his shoulders relaxed.

Yes, when this flesh and heart may fail, and mortal life shall cease:

I shall possess, within the veil, a life of joy and peace.

The first part of that had come true. But that meant Grandpa was gone. What joy and peace was Grizz supposed to find in that?

"Psst." Dani passed him the binoculars. "Intruder on the fourth perimeter. He's got a long-bow like yours."

Third, but he wasn't going to correct her. He homed in on the location Dani had pointed out.

Not good. Why would this guy have a long-bow?

Grizz's stomach tightened. He and Dani were being hunted. The men from the compound were on a mission to eradicate any evidence of their operation in the woods. And Dani was the loose end they needed to tie up.

He scanned the area and saw another camouflaged man to his right. Now they had two tangos to contend with.

"Wait." Dani grabbed the binoculars from Grizz and pointed them to the northern sky. "Do you hear that sound?"

Grizz listened and then heard the thumping of rotor blades. A helicopter.

His crew. Grizz knew the sound of the rescue helo, and he confirmed it through the scope of his rifle, just to make sure it wasn't the commandos trying to bring in reinforcements.

The red-and-white chopper veered around the side of a mountain and came into view. His energy renewed. Help was on the horizon.

Grizz watched through his scope. The man lurking in the shadows retreated farther into the woods, away from the cabin.

Perfect. Grizz was counting on the helicopter forcing a retreat.

"And now we make a run for it." He turned to Dani. "Go inside and pack up the backpacks with water and supplies. I'm going to watch to make sure our visitors back off so we can get away and meet the helicopter."

Dani raced into the loft. Grizz watched for movement in the trees and spotted the same man, now heading away from his property.

"Perfect." Their window of escape opened, and Grizz would save the battle for another day. These guys would return with reinforcements. This was probably a scouting operation.

Grizz dashed into the outhouse and down the stairs. Dani was waiting by the ATVs with the backpack on, ready to leave.

"Let's go." Grizz started the vehicle and opened the garage door with a remote. The well-oiled track muffled the sound, but it still would be loud enough for anyone close by to hear.

"The men look like they are retreating, but I know where the landing spot should be. It will take about ten minutes, and I'm hopeful we won't cross paths with these mercenaries. They should be heading into the woods and toward their shelter, which will give us some breathing room."

Dani jumped on the back of his four-wheeler and slipped her arms around his waist. "I trust you," he heard her whisper over the rumbling motor.

Trust? When had they crossed over into that kind of relationship where they trusted each other? Did he trust Dani not to sell him out for a story? Could he open his heart up even a crack to let her in?

He focused on the mission ahead and pointed the four-wheeler toward the marked path that ran behind his property. Trees whipped by them while the cool headwind riffled through Dani's hair, sending strands of blonde flying.

After a few minutes, the dirt trail ended, and a green field sprawled across an inlet.

"There. I see the helicopter." Dani pointed over

Grizz's shoulder, and he relaxed a little. His eyes hadn't stopped roaming every hill and tree they'd passed, looking for any signs of trouble.

A small river flowed through the relatively flat land. The rescue copter rested in the center of the field, waiting for their arrival.

Grizz pulled up next to the helicopter and took in a fresh breath of air. "Our rescue has arrived, Dani. We're going to get you out of here with that evidence."

She jumped off the bike and patted her jeans pocket. "I'll be glad to get rid of this and let the authorities take over."

Recognizable faces emerged from the helicopter. Sanchez, Kane, and Saxon jumped from the opened door and ran like they were being chased by a bear. The speed of their approach shot daggers of ice through Grizz's veins.

What had them so spooked?

"We've got company." Kane slowed down long enough to point to a spot on a hill, overlooking the river. He passed a radio to Grizz and took off running into a copse of trees.

Grizz saw the glint of metal from the RPG launcher on a camouflaged man's shoulder. "Dani, hop back. We've got to get out of here."

A deafening boom rang through his ears. The helo exploded into an orange-and-red fireball.

SIX

DANI'S DEATH GRIP AROUND GRIZZ'S waist strained every muscle in her arms, but she refused to let go. He tore through the woods on the four-wheeler while his teammates scattered on foot.

These men were after her, and they'd just taken out her source of rescue.

She dared to glance over her shoulder and saw the skeletal remains of their escape vehicle, now an empty hull filled with flames and black smoke.

"What are we going to do?" She yelled in Grizz's ear to be heard over the whipping wind and roar of the motor.

"I'm heading to the cabin. We should be safe in the outhouse while we regroup. At least we have a radio now. I can let the others know."

Dani prayed these men didn't follow them. Grizz remained on high alert, looking for trouble. The bumpy ride took less than ten minutes to return Grizz's property. He pulled the ATV into the garage and shut the door.

"I didn't see anyone following us." Grizz held out his hand to assist Dani off the vehicle. "But they'll be back. They know we don't have a lot of options for a place to hide."

Grizz radioed his location to the others and contacted base camp to give them an update. "My commander is going to find Rio and let him know what's going on. They're going to send help, but the winds are picking up, so we may have to wait it out."

Dani grasped her hands to keep them from trembling. "This mess is all my fault. Those men are after me. I know too much."

Grizz walked toward her and wrapped his arms around her in a hug. His solid frame enveloped her and gave her a brief respite from the storm.

"I'm going to make sure you get off this mountain, Dani. We'll get that evidence to the FBI. We have a radio and can get in touch with Rio. We'll make a plan when the others arrive."

He let go, and a chill washed over her. She missed his warmth.

"I can help with food." Dani busied herself in the kitchen area. She found some of Grizz's famous venison stew in the freezer and began to heat it on the two-burner stove.

Grizz's radio clicked twice. "They're here." He headed up the stairs to the outhouse door, unbolted it, and let the two men and one woman in. They were covered in dirt and soot, but at least they'd made it out of that explosion in time.

"Dani, let me introduce you to the crew."

Oh, she remembered this *crew*. The snickers and stares came back to her from their first encounter. Would they still give her the cold shoulder now that her information had been proven true?

Grizz turned to the woman in the hotshot-logoed T-shirt and dirt-covered jeans. "This is Sanchez. And these two stragglers are Kane and Saxon."

Dani nodded. "It's nice to officially meet you all."

Saxon looked at the floor. The man appeared to be in his early thirties, his long, dark hair tied in a man bun, his face sporting an even darker beard. "Yeah, about that. I'm sorry we weren't very hospitable on our first meeting. I'm glad Grizz found you."

Kane also apologized while Sanchez watched but said nothing. What was it like to be a female hotshot? Dani had experience being a lone female in a male-dominated career.

She stowed her emotional baggage into the recesses of her heart and accepted the sincere apologies. She hadn't been the nicest either when she'd demanded that they take her into the woods on a hunch. "I just appreciate your rescue attempt. You put your life on the line coming to our aid. How did you know we were in trouble?"

Saxon shrugged. "Grizz never returned with you. And with the cell phones down, Skye was worried and sent us looking."

"I can't believe we were attacked again. In our own backyard." Kane grabbed a bottle of water that Dani had placed on the counter. "We need to debrief. What is going down on Copper Mountain? What's the plan? Because I'm not a fan of being trapped here with deranged gunmen roaming the woods. Ones that have some massive weaponry. An RPG? Really?"

Saxon spun in a circle. "I guess if I'm going to be trapped, this bunker in the side of the mountain is better than pitching a tent outside. Nice digs you've got here, Grizz. But I'd also like to know the full story of what we're up against before I sleep with one eye open."

"I'm sure you're all familiar with Grizz's outhouse. There's plenty of room for us all."

They stared at Dani like she had three heads. Sanchez said, "His what?"

She glanced at Grizz and found him looking at the ground. She was the only one who'd been here? "You've never seen Grizz's place?"

"He's never invited us," Sanchez said. "But to be fair, he spends most of his time at base camp."

Dani moved to the kitchen area. "Well, how about I dish us up some venison stew, and we can debrief."

She poured the stew into coffee mugs, and Grizz pulled out some camping chairs for everyone to have a seat. Dani served everyone and took a seat, her hands wrapped around the warm mug.

"I hate to ask this," Sanchez said, her voice soft, "but what happened to the man you were with, Dani?"

Her heart sank. She took a deep breath, shoving back the tears that threatened to flow. "We found the compound. Josh and I saw the guns and weapons. They have some sort of chemical plant in the middle of their highly guarded camp. But Josh decided to head down the mountain and was captured. They killed him. Dumped his body in the woods."

Sanchez never broke eye contact, her intense stare giving Dani goosebumps. "Someone needs to stop these men."

Grizz put his mug on one of his infamous stump end tables. "Dani has proof. Josh had taken pictures and video. We have the SIM card and need to get it to Rio. The FBI needs to shut this place down. I can head back to my cabin and grab my laptop so you can see what we're up against."

Dani gathered the cups while Grizz headed through his tunnel, returning with his dinosaur laptop. She took the SIM card out of her pocket and gave it to Grizz. The three hotshots gathered around to view the evidence. Dani didn't need to relive it again, so she paced behind them.

Grizz paused the video. "This guy. Do you recognize him from somewhere?"

Saxon zoomed in on the guy's face. "Jeremiah Redding." He glanced at Kane, and they shared a hard look for a second. "Rio has an alert out for him. His entire family is bad news." Dani caught the still frame of the dark-blond guy with the snake tattoo running up his neck.

Kane studied the frozen screen. "The guy in the background. Is that . . ."

"Yep. We think Senator Deville is part of this group. It explains how they've managed to move around undetected. Not to mention there's video of a stockpile of weapons."

Saxon leaned in closer. "That explains where the RPG came from."

Grizz hit play and the video continued.

The hostage came into view and Sanchez gasped. "He's here."

"Who is?" Grizz's head whipped to Sanchez. The woman's face had paled, and her finger trembled as she pointed at the screen.

"Doctor Cortez." Kane put his hand on Sanchez's shoulder in a protective gesture.

Dani frowned. "Who?"

Sanchez said, "My father."

Grizz refrained from punching the steel wall of his outhouse. No one messed with his teammates. Or Dani. Not on his watch.

"We have to go." Sanchez's determined gaze darted around the room. "We'll take one of your vehicles. If there's a chance my father is still there, I must find him."

Kane didn't leave Sanchez's side. "We need to wait for backup. And daylight. We don't know if these men are watching this place. It's too risky to leave."

Grizz had noted the connection these two shared. If anyone could talk some sense into Sanchez, it was Kane.

Saxon looked at Grizz. "You have weapons, I assume. And transportation. I say we go on the offensive. Before they shut down camp and bug out."

Grizz shook his head. "These men are relentless and well-armed. I've only identified two of them. Plus, we know that a senator is involved with this group. Let's face it, we don't know what we're up against. I agree with Kane. We wait for backup."

Tension blanketed the room. Dani cleared her throat. This woman was as unpredictable as the Alaskan weather. What would she say to a bunch of hotshots ready to take matters into their own hands—especially Sanchez?

"I have a question." All eyes zipped to Dani. "Does anyone actually know our friend Grizz's first name?"

Grizz groaned. "That's your burning question?"

"I—I actually have no idea." Sanchez shrugged. "He's always just been Grizz."

"Someone has to know." Kane shook his head. "But I don't."

Saxon squinted. "I want to say Phil. Or Peter. Or it starts with a P or an R maybe—"

"Wait, how do any of us not know?" Sanchez relaxed her shoulders, and Grizz was impressed with Dani's ability to change the subject.

Dani sat back in her camping chair. "Seems like he's concealed his identity well. Good thing I'm an award-winning investigative reporter up for the challenge."

Kane smirked. "Looks like Grizz has met his match."

Grizz felt the heat rising up his neck. He hated being the center of attention more than he hated his first name. But if it gave Sanchez and Saxon pause before rushing headfirst into danger, he'd take the brunt of their teasing.

Dani kept egging on his crew. She was good at getting people to talk. "At least give me some ammunition. Who's got a good Grizz story? I pay cash for the best story. Once I return to civilization and find an ATM."

Sanchez showed a hint of a smile and sat next to Dani.

Grizz shook his head and sat in the chair across from the women. "They wouldn't dare."

"Well . . ." Saxon helped himself to another bowl of stew and then plopped into a camping chair next to Grizz that wasn't meant to hold the muscular man's weight. "Let's see. There's the time we had to rescue Grizz from a tree. He thought he'd cut down the tree from the top down, but it doesn't work out so well when you forget to gas up your chain saw."

"No way. Stuck?" Dani was enjoying this a little too much, but he savored her smile. This was the first time she'd let loose and had fun around him.

Saxon guffawed. "Stuck in the tree like the proverbial cat. We had to get a ladder truck to get him down."

"Or what about the time Grizz met his match against that moose?" Sanchez nodded to Grizz. "He was a quarter mile behind us, and the next thing I see is this blur run past me. I've never seen anyone run that fast."

"That was one ticked-off moose." Grizz soaked in the camaraderie and light-hearted banter, letting it erase a bit of the tension from the past twenty-four hours. But he couldn't completely let his guard down.

Dani leaned close to Sanchez. "Tell us about your father. How is he caught up in all this?"

The others fell silent. Sanchez wasn't known for being talkative, especially when it came to her story. At least, Grizz didn't know much of it.

Sanchez sighed. "He was kidnapped fifteen years ago. I've been searching for him for years, but . . ."

No one spoke or moved. Sanchez's grief was palatable, engulfing the room. Grizz kept his voice low. "Is anyone looking into this?"

Sanchez shook her head. "To my knowledge, they've written him off, but I refuse to lose another parent. And now we have proof he's out there. We have to find him." Her throat bobbed as she sucked down her emotions, a move she'd obviously perfected.

Dani gave Grizz a small nod to indicate she wouldn't press Sanchez for additional information. The dazed look in Sanchez's eyes told him it was time to switch gears.

Grizz stood. "I recommend we get some rest for a few hours. I've got plenty of places for us to crash for the night. Even have some sleeping bags and pillows if anyone wants to rest. I've got my lookout and will take the first night watch."

Saxon snorted. "Do you think any of us will sleep? I'm going to patrol the area, see what I can find."

Grizz nodded. "Be careful. I've got some trip wires set up to alert me to intruders."

"Of course you do."

After receiving a quick rundown of the perimeter system, Saxon gave him a mock salute before heading out.

Grizz grabbed some sleeping bags out of a storage bin where he kept his camping gear. He handed Dani the bedding and pointed to his perch above the property. "I'll be up there on overwatch."

"Copy that." She gave him a weak smile, and he prayed she'd take the opportunity to rest. The dark circles under her eyes betrayed her fatigue.

"Dani, please don't go rogue on me. I know you have a big heart and want to help Sanchez as well as avenge Josh's death by stopping these terrorists, but we have to wait for resources. Tomorrow we'll be able to get the evidence to Rio. Until then, please rest."

She nodded. "You can trust me. I'm following your lead. I'm willing to admit I'm out of my element. And you've kept me safe this far."

There was that word again. *Trust.* The one thing Grizz didn't give easily. Could he trust her not to race headfirst in harm's way?

Kane and Sanchez remained in the camping chairs. Sanchez stared into space, and Kane acted as the overprotective brother. The Trouble Boys had always looked after Sanchez. They'd become a family, though Grizz speculated that Kane's feelings were a little less like a brother and more romantically inclined. But Kane would throat punch him if he dared suggest it.

Grizz watched Dani curl up in the corner with the sleeping bag, and he headed to his loft. He used his night-vision goggles to watch for any signs of life. Darkness blanketed the mountainside due to the storm clouds churning through the sky. An occasional streak of lighting flashed, temporarily blinding him. He spotted Saxon in his second perimeter.

Grizz's eyelids grew heavy. Maybe he should go inside and get some rest. Tomorrow, Rio should be able to reach them.

Thunder rumbled in the distance.

Wait. Not thunder.

That was the sound of the garage door opening and closing. Grizz tore into the loft and flew down the stairs. He stared at the empty space where his motorcycle had been previously parked.

The sting of betrayal slapped him in the face. He moved in a circle around the middle of the outhouse garage. No sign of Sanchez or Kane.

But the biggest kick in the teeth was that Dani had left with them.

So much for trust.

SEVEN

GRIZZ'S GROWL REVERBERATED through the bathroom. Dani finished washing her face and cracked the door open to peek out, afraid of what she'd find.

She'd heard Kane and Sanchez whispering. Dani had pretended to sleep while they'd opened the garage door and rolled Grizz's motorcycle out.

Should she have stopped them? Part of her had wanted to jump into action with them, but she knew Grizz wouldn't approve. And Grizz's approval meant something to her.

Not to mention that she wanted to personally hand the SIM card to Rio. Her job was to protect the evidence.

Dani watched Grizz pace the room, flexing his

hands into fists at his side. Saxon returned from his patrol.

"She left." Grizz mumbled something she couldn't hear.

"We knew Sanchez was a flight risk. I wasn't close enough to stop her. But Kane should have intervened. She must have worn him down."

"Not Sanchez. Dani."

"Dani's gone too? I didn't see her leave."

Grizz huffed. "That girl is going to be the death of me. She'd trade her safety for a story any day."

Was that what Grizz thought of her? Some career-driven, heartless woman?

"I knew I couldn't trust her." Those words cut through her like a knife. Grizz actually thought she'd run off to chase a story, exploiting Sanchez's need to rescue her father.

Heat raced through her. Before she could second-guess her actions, she flung the bathroom door open. It clattered against the metal wall, echoing through the outhouse.

She marched toward Grizz, hands on hips. Saxon took ten steps backward and disappeared up the stairs toward the loft.

Dani pointed her finger right into Grizz's chest. "You really think I'd sell you out for a story? That I don't care about finding Sanchez's father? I can't believe you think I'm some kind of heartless monster that cares more about work than people."

She bit back the tears. Because there was some truth to his accusation. Her ambitions had dragged Josh across the country. Her persistence had gotten him killed.

"No—I—grrr." He threw up his arms in frustration and paced.

She waited for him to simmer down.

"Dani, when I saw the motorcycle gone, along with Sanchez and Kane, I assumed the worst. For that, I'm sorry. I misjudged you. Again."

Thunder rattled through the outhouse, and rain pelted the structure. Dani sank into one of the camping chairs. "I get why you'd think that of me. I refuse to get complacent or lower my guard. Those men killed Josh. The world needs to hear his story. It's my fault—"

"Just stop, Dani." He sank into the chair next to her and placed his hand on hers. Electricity sparked through her. "What happened to Josh wasn't your fault. Sometimes things are out of your control."

There was that word again. *Control.* What had that Bible verse said? *I can do all things through Christ who strengthens me.* She sighed. "Second place is still losing."

Grizz squeezed her hand, and she relished the warmth of his touch. "Tell me why you think this." His husky voice was soft, laced with compassion—the words urging her to bare her soul to this man that had crashed into her world and turned it upside down.

"I can't lose. My father drilled that into my head as a child. I was on my way to becoming an Olympic gymnast until I fell. I hurt myself and lost my ranking. My dad moved on to coach my sister. All because I lost. It's his voice that pushes me to win at all costs."

Grizz sighed. "Isn't that tiring, having to push so hard all the time?"

"It's lonely." Just having him in such close proximity reminded her of how alone she'd been. When was the last time she'd made time for a date? "I just thought that's the way it was supposed to be. Work as hard as you can. Make it to the top. Do it all on your own so no one can take credit for your success."

"But what happens if you . . . I don't know . . . find yourself stuck in a tree and your friends have to come rescue you?"

She laughed at his grimace.

"I guess I'd have to find a way down on my own. I don't have a lot of friends that would come rushing in the way your hotshot crew does. Most of my friendships are superficial or people I'm competing against. Most reporters are just waiting in the wings for me to fail so they can swoop in and take my spot."

Grizz shook his head. "You could have the same kind of relationships too, if you let people help you."

What would that be like to have friends that stepped in when she needed help? A few of her supposed friends had dropped her once she had the stigma of that bad report.

He rubbed circles on the back of her hand with his thumb, and she leaned her head against his shoulder.

Lightning lit up the room through the one window by the loft, and the distraction shattered her illusion of safety. This couldn't happen. No way was she getting cozy with this mountain man. Despite the cool temperatures that had settled in the outhouse, her face flushed. She hoped Grizz couldn't see.

"Hot chocolate." She stood, severing their connection. "I found some packets in the kitchen. I need a warm drink." She moved to the kitchen area and found a pot to boil some water.

Grizz watched in silence until the radio crackled.

"Grizz. Come in."

He jumped up from the chair and snatched the radio from the counter. "It's Rio. Finally." He punched the button on the radio. "What's the plan, Rio?"

"We can't get to your place. Road is washed out. Can you make your way to your cousin's cabin? That road is passable. In the meantime, I'm calling all agencies to send backup. We'll stop these guys and get you and Dani off the mountain. Do you think you can make it?"

"We'll do our best."

The kettle whistle made Dani jump. Her nerves were fried, but at least now help was near.

But another hissing sound gave her pause. It wasn't from the boiling water. Grizz stood alert, eyes wide.

Saxon rushed into the outhouse. "We've got company. And looks like they brought fire power. Two men just used longbows to light up the forest around your cabin. They're trying to smoke us out."

How long could Grizz keep Dani safe? She had

the power to take down this secret militia group and a senator.

"Dani, stay inside." Grizz and Saxon scrambled up the stairs to the loft, then stepped out onto the wooden deck. Sunlight peeked through the clouds, but it was the light from the fire that sparked his anger.

These men were about to burn his grandfather's legacy to the ground.

A fire on the east side of his property churned and ate up the trees and shrubs in its path. If left unchecked, it would head straight for Grizz's cabin. At least the rain had dampened the ground to slow down the spread of destruction.

Grizz turned to Saxon. "Apparently these men want us alive, or they would have just taken out the cabin."

"They want that evidence. And Dani. They're tying up all loose ends. But for some reason, they want the journalist alive."

"We need to put out that fire, Saxon."

Saxon pointed toward the left of the property, and Grizz grabbed his binoculars for a closer look. Two men, perched on a rock overlooking the west side of Grizz's yard, watched his cabin through their rifle scopes.

"The two men are back." Saxon used the scope

of his rifle to view the area. "I heard Rio on the radio. I think you and Dani need to run. I'll work on putting out the fire before it gets to your cabin. I found your equipment and hose. I'm going in."

"By yourself? It's a trap, Saxon. We need backup." Grizz scanned the area again with binoculars. Flames licked the second perimeter around his land. All of his grandfather's work—and Grizz's own work—would be decimated if the fire spread.

Grizz flexed his fists. No way was he running, but he had to get that SIM card to Rio.

If only Sanchez and Kane hadn't run off. Yes, he understood why Sanchez had run off in hopes of finding her father. But she'd gone rogue and left Grizz, Saxon, and Dani trapped. He'd give Sanchez and Kane a piece of his mind when they resurfaced—

A shot from a high-powered rifle hissed through the air. Grizz trained his binoculars on the two men. "Someone fired a shot, but it wasn't our trespassers."

Saxon and Grizz watched as another bullet hit the tree right behind the men, sending shards of bark flying. The men packed up their gear and bolted, sinking farther into the forest, away from the property.

Grizz scanned the area. Who had been shooting?

The garage door opened, and Grizz and Saxon raced from the loft just in time to see Kane and Sanchez drive up on Grizz's motorcycle.

Kane hadn't parked the bike before he began shouting orders. "Sanchez and I can fight the blaze with your hose and equipment. Saxon, you watch from above and take out those men if they return. Grizz, doesn't your cousin have a cabin around here? I remember reading an article about it, and it's not too far from here. You could take Dani and head for Mike's place. We'll meet you there once we deal with the fire and these intruders."

And just like that, his team kicked into action like a well-rehearsed dance troupe, everyone knowing their parts.

Dani hopped on the back of the four-wheeler. "I've already packed supplies ready to go."

Saxon headed to the loft with his rifle slung over his shoulder. Kane headed out the outhouse door toward the cabin, where Grizz had a hose.

Grizz caught Sanchez before she headed to help Kane. "Did you find anything? I'm assuming you headed to the compound."

"We never made it. We stopped for some surveillance and discovered the men's hiding spot. I'm sorry we couldn't stop them before they shot that fiery arrow. At least it's not your cabin."

The sadness in Sanchez's eyes squeezed Grizz's heart. "We're going to find your father."

"And we'll defend your property," Sanchez said, then rushed outside after Kane.

Grizz took his spot on the ATV, Dani wrapped her arms around his waist, and he hit the button on the remote control to raise the door.

The crack of a rifle indicated that Saxon was laying some cover for them to escape. Grizz whipped his head around, looking for any signs of danger, but with the fighting and fire closer to his cabin, the outhouse remained unscathed.

He followed the dirt path through the woods until he hit the gravel path that would traverse the side of the mountain toward Mike Grizz's cabin.

"How far away is this place?" Dani asked over the rush of wind whipping in his ear.

"About a fifteen-minute ride."

Sunlight streaked through the clouds in the sky. This would have been a beautiful day for hiking. Dani would love his favorite lookout spot that ran along a ridge over a valley. Maybe he could take her after this was all over—

Was he making plans in his head that extended

beyond their current situation? Dani's Alaskan adventure wasn't permanent. She'd return to her big-city digs the second this story closed. She'd be on to the next big thing.

Which left no room for Grizz.

Loose gravel crunched under the tires. The motor revved as they climbed a steep hill.

Click. Click.

"No, no, no." Grizz hit the throttle, but their vehicle chugged to a stop.

"What's wrong, Grizz?" They both jumped off. Grizz walked around the stalled vehicle and checked the engine.

He groaned. "Fuel line has a leak. I don't have any tools with me to fix it, and I don't like being out in the open like this."

Grizz turned in a circle. Nothing but trees and mountain peaks all around. "This path leads to my cousin's place. I think we should walk. It's probably only another two miles."

"I'm up for another adventure. Walking it is." Dani tightened the backpack straps around her shoulders. She was still wearing his sister's gray sweatshirt.

"You're not cold?"

She shrugged. "I seem to be getting used to the

weather. At least I packed water and food for us. Good thinking, since we broke down."

"Well, let's hit the road." Grizz's eyes roamed the area, and he occasionally checked behind them. If the men had heard the engine rumble, they could have followed. But hopefully Saxon was keeping them busy.

"Where exactly are we going? You said your cousin has a cabin?"

"My definition of *cabin* and Mike's are very different. Mike and his wife Seraphina bought the place and renovated it. It's more like a resort than a cabin. But he's working in Montana, so he won't mind us crashing there while we hide out from deranged gunmen."

Dani stopped short. "Wait. Mike Grizz? As in the television producer? *Go Wild with Grizz*? *Survivor Quest*? That Mike Grizz?"

Grizz nodded. "That's my cousin."

"I love that show."

He started walking again. "You're living that show. You've got way more survival instincts than you give yourself credit for."

She shrugged off the compliment and changed the subject. "I can see why you love living in the mountains. It's beautiful. But if we have two more miles to walk, I need a distraction. Mind if I ask you a personal question?"

Warning bells clanged in Grizz's mind. He needed to tread carefully when it came to this reporter. She had a way of getting to the heart of the matter. "I'm not telling you my first name."

"Yeah, I know. You don't trust me enough to reveal your biggest secret. But what I want to know is whether you trust me. After all we've been through, do you really think I'd sell you out the first chance I get so I can land a big story?"

Grizz ran a hand through his hair. "I jumped to the wrong conclusion. But it's hard to trust anyone after you've been betrayed as many times as I have. You learn who you can count on. It's hard to blindly accept that others will be there for you in the end."

"I get what it's like to have people stab you in the back." She moved a tree branch out of her way like it was second nature for her to be traipsing through the woods of Alaska.

"I've got my team. I know they'll be there for me. That's all I need."

"But isn't it lonely living in the woods by yourself? I know you live on base most of the time. But in the offseason? It's so remote that your team doesn't even visit. What about your family?"

"My sister visits with her kids, but I like having my own space. My mom moved to Anchorage after my dad passed away. I don't see her as much as I should. Once Grandpa was gone, my family scattered." He kicked a pebble. His grandfather had been his rock. "When I was ten, my grandfather promised to always be there for me, whenever I needed him. I loved visiting the cabin in the summer. But then cancer made him renege on his promise."

Dani swiped her face. Tears or dirt? He couldn't tell. Maybe a mix of both.

"That's so hard to process when you're young. But you've kept his legacy alive by keeping his cabin."

A hawk screeched in the distance. He knew Dani was gearing up for more personal questions, and he really had nowhere to go.

She cleared her throat. "Anyone else in your life? A girlfriend, perhaps?"

A name popped into his head. *Candice Jackson.*

He looked at the ground and watched his feet stir up dust from the gravel. "I did have a relationship that ended badly. Things were great at first, but then she decided she wanted more. I had even agreed to move to the Lower 48 with her. Give her everything she wanted. But—"

But what? He would have given up his life for her. And she'd taken everything he had offered and wanted more.

He ran a hand through his hair. "Let's just say I wasn't enough for Candice. She wanted to live in a big city, with all the action and excitement. I was a little too woodsy for her tastes. I discovered that she'd been seeing a good friend of mine from high school. A friend that had gone to law school and made a name for himself in Miami, Florida. She left without even a goodbye."

Dani grabbed his hand and gave it a squeeze. "Thank you for sharing your story. I understand why you have a hard time trusting people after someone like Candice stomps on your heart."

She paused, as if gathering her words. "I guess I can see why you misjudged me. I'm from the city, and you were burned by someone who didn't appreciate you for who you are. And maybe I'm a little like her, but I don't think you should have to give up everything for someone you care about. There has to be some compromise."

Grizz zeroed in on the fact that Dani hadn't let his hand go. They looked like school kids, skipping through the woods hand in hand. But he didn't hate it.

What would she think of him if she knew the

truth—how he'd trusted the wrong person, putting his Army teammates in direct danger? He'd told her that Josh's death wasn't on her, but it was hard to get over Kyle's death when Grizz's orders had ended his life.

A twig snapped behind them. Grizz turned and saw the source of the noise. "Time to pick up the pace."

EIGHT

THE CITY-GIRL INSTINCT IN DANI made her want to scream and run, but she kept her cool.

Somewhat.

She only stumbled twice in her adrenaline-fueled sprint down the hill, arms flailing and hair flying in the breeze.

Grizz's laughter filled her ears. She slowed and dared to look over her shoulder at the momma black bear with her cubs, marching across the path they'd just occupied. This up-close-and-personal-with-nature adventure was miles out of her comfort zone, yet seeing the baby bears playing and rolling across the leaves and gravel sent a thrill through her. When would she ever get to experience something like this again? Or share the moment with this ultimate wild tour guide? She'd held back tears when he'd told her his story. The loss and hurt he'd carried for so long struck a chord within her soul.

Because a similar melody had played as the backdrop of her own life.

Grizz slowed when they were a safe distance away. "That was a little too close for comfort. But we're almost there." He pointed through the trees to a cleared area that opened up into sprawling fields of green grass. "Welcome to Grizz Manor."

"Yes. You and your cousin do have very different ideas about the meaning of *cabin*." Dani gaped at the size of the mansion ahead of her. Acres of cleared land held a paved driveway and a house the size of a hotel.

It took another ten minutes to get down the hill and arrive at the front of the estate. Grizz punched a six-digit code into the keypad, and a gate creaked open.

"This place looks like some high-end resort. Not a summer house." The two-story home consisted of exposed and unpainted tan wood beams, giving it a rustic vibe. But there was nothing roughing it with this cabin.

Grizz waved his hands as if to showcase the

house. "Five bedrooms. A deck with breathtaking views. Oh, and a hot tub."

After another keypad entry, Grizz opened the front door.

Dani walked through the foyer and gasped. The spacious living room that led onto a wooden-deck balcony overlooked a lake with mountain peaks as a backdrop. Floor-to-ceiling windows outfitted the back wall, leaving her spellbound. Sunlight glistened off the water, helping her regain some of that fleeting peace.

"This place is amazing." She touched a glass sconce over the brick fireplace complete with marble mantel.

Grizz snorted. "Mike doesn't have an outhouse."

Dani laughed. "Yeah, you've got him beat there. I can't get over how beautiful this place is, inside and out. We don't have views like this in DC."

The wooden deck overlooked the expansive backyard and lake. A canoe lay upside down in front of the blue water. The mountain range hemmed them in, creating a postcard picture, despite the drizzly rain. The patio was covered, at least.

Dani shook her head. "I don't know, Grizz. I

kind of like your place better. This place has all of the amenities, but your place has heart."

"Heart?"

"Yes. Character. Your cabin isn't going to be the focus of a reality show, but it's home. I'm just praying your crew can get that fire put out."

"Agreed. Hopefully they'll make it here soon," said Grizz.

"Do you think your cousin has coffee? Would he mind me helping myself to some liquid sustenance?"

"I'm sure he won't mind. I'll explain it all to him. His wife likes me." He shot her a quirky grin that made her bite her lip to keep from laughing.

The kitchen had all of the latest gadgets, not to mention two stoves and a well-stocked refrigerator. "They must have just left. There's plenty of food in the fridge. I can make us some breakfast." Grizz sat on the barstool at the kitchen island. "They have a cleaning company that will shut the place down for the winter, so we must have arrived just in time."

Dani opened a cabinet and found several cans of Spam. She scrunched her nose at the canned meat. "Really?" She held one of the cans out for Grizz to inspect.

"I wouldn't have taken Mike as a Spam kind

of guy, but if you find some eggs, that's a mighty fine breakfast by my standards."

"I guess I'm up for another Alaskan adventure then." She grabbed a pan and worked on cooking up the eggs, relieved to also have found some bacon in the refrigerator. Dani dropped the spatula in her hand at the sound of the intercom buzzing. She checked at the lit built-in screen in the wall. "It's the front gate."

Grizz moved to a panel and hit a few buttons. "It's Saxon, Kane, and Sanchez."

Grizz moved to the front door and returned with his crew.

"Don't worry, we've got food for everyone." Dani started dishing out plates. "I hope everyone likes Spam and eggs."

"At this point, any hot meal is welcome." Saxon sat at the countertop, his hair sticking out at all angles from his man bun.

"We managed to put out the fire." Kane took a plate and sat next to Saxon. "But we lost the men. They retreated, however, we don't know if they headed to their compound or went looking for you two."

Saxon nodded. "Once we're done eating, we'll take turns patrolling Mike's place to look out for signs of trouble. How far away is Rio?"

Grizz pulled out the radio and checked on Rio.

Rio responded. "I'm about two hours from arrival. I've had to run this mission up the chain of command and request backup. Stay where you are. I'll be there soon."

The radio made Dani realize that she'd had no contact with the outside world. "Does anyone have a working phone? I need to call my boss and let him know the situation."

Kane shook his head. "Lightning took out a cell tower. Our radio is satellite. But Rio should be able to help you once he arrives."

After eating, everyone dispersed. The men were going to rotate turns on patrol. They'd decided that Kane and Saxon would take the first shift while Grizz rested in one of Mike's spare bedrooms.

Dani cleaned up the breakfast dishes, sticking them in the dishwasher and turning it on. Sanchez sat at the countertop bar and watched.

Time to put on her investigator hat. Maybe a little girl talk was in order. It wouldn't hurt for Dani to find out more about the woman's missing father. Dani couldn't turn off her inquisitive side that easily. "How long have you worked with Grizz?"

"Cut the small talk, Dani." Sanchez ran her

fingers through her long, dark wavy hair. "What's going on between you and Grizz? The man is a natural-born protector, but he can't take his eyes off you. Spill."

A full-on inferno engulfed her from head to toe. She channeled all of her energy into the cup of coffee she'd just poured herself. "There's nothing going on between us. No more than two strangers being trapped on the side of the mountain."

"Riiiiight," Sanchez said, with three extra syllables added for emphasis.

"Do you grill all the women in Grizz's life like this?"

"What women?" Sanchez laughed. "In the time that I've known Grizz, he's been the perpetual bachelor. But I have a feeling that if any woman could handle a hothead like Grizz, it's you."

"Handle? I'm lucky to be alive. Besides, I'm not made for the wilds of Alaska. I'm a city girl at heart."

Sanchez shook her head. "You're a lot stronger than you give yourself credit for. We judged you, and you proved us all wrong. You might not fight fires, but you're no damsel in distress either. You hold your own."

What a compliment. Sanchez was the true hero, saving lives and thriving in a predominantly male-dominated job. But this couldn't be about Grizz.

The subject of Grizz made Dani shift from one foot to the other, and she swirled the contents of her mug. "Grizz isn't even my type. Could you imagine me, living here in the middle of nowhere? Or him in DC?"

Sanchez watched Dani without saying anything.

Dani couldn't hold her tongue. "I mean, he's got a softer side than most men, not to mention he cooks and cleans. It's surprising, really. But I couldn't fall for a mountain man. Yes, he's really good-looking. But my career keeps me so busy."

Sanchez rolled her eyes.

"I'm so used to being on my own. I don't know how to slow down, take the time to get to know someone. Most men I meet have ulterior motives. Grizz is the first man that doesn't expect me to be perfect." Dani continued. "I keep catching glimpses of a future. One where I'm not a reporter. Where I don't have to perform. Where I don't have to kill myself to stay in first place." She sighed. "Would it hurt to slow down, let others in? It's not a sign of quitting. It's more of a way to enjoy the things I have without racing to the next thing. To savor the moment."

Dani poured more coffee—not that she needed the caffeine. She was amped up. "I know my weakness. I don't know when to quit. But Grizz keeps showing up at the right time to save me from the decisions I've made. So maybe I do need a partner. Someone that I know has my back. Like your team. You're all there for each other. I envy that."

Sanchez opened her mouth to say something, but Dani couldn't lose her train of thought. "I need relationships. Not people taking up space. Not assignments or awards. I need true friendships." She looked Sanchez in the eyes. "Wow. I'm glad we had this conversation. You've given me a lot to think about."

Sanchez gave her a puzzled look. "Glad I could help."

While a load had been lifted from Dani's shoulders, she was still a journalist. "What's the plan to rescue your father? I want to help."

Sanchez's face tightened. "All I can do is wait for Rio at the moment. And according to Kane, it's apparently in God's hands. I shouldn't have tried to go out on my own last night. Who knows if my father is even still at the camp?"

God again?

If only Dani could get on board with a God who came to her rescue. But she wasn't waiting around for a God who may or may not show up. She'd take care of herself.

Where was Rio? The FBI agent should have been here by now.

Grizz sat on the white couch in his cousin's overly decorated castle. Definitely not Grizz's tastes.

But Dani liked his cabin better. Take that, Mike Grizz and your fancy five-bedroom monstrosity.

Not that he'd complain. The place was providing them with nice shelter until Rio could arrive and collect the data.

Grizz had showered and borrowed some of Mike's clothes.

Dani came downstairs and sat by him on the couch. A little too close, but he didn't mind. He wanted her as close as possible. He could smell the coconut shampoo, her damp hair now a shade darker than her usual blonde.

"I borrowed some of your sister-in-law's clothes. When I get home, I'm sending everyone gift cards to replace all the things I borrowed . . .

and destroyed. I snagged your sister's sweatshirt on a tree branch, and now it has a hole."

Her fresh jeans and long-sleeved tee hugged her curves in all the right places. The bright color of the shirt made her blue eyes pop.

Get your head in the game, Grizz. "Ah, it's not a problem. Melanie and Seraphina would be happy to help, knowing the danger you've endured."

"I'm glad you have them in your life, Grizz. I know it's hard for you to trust people after what happened." She curled her legs up under her on the sofa and leaned in closer to him. "You don't talk about it, but I assume you served in the military. And you know me—nosy reporter. Did you serve in Afghanistan?"

He nodded, trying to swallow the golf-ball-sized lump forming in his throat.

Images of his friend Kyle pummeled his memories. If only he hadn't blindly accepted that faulty intel. If only—

Dani's hand rested on his bicep. "Tell me what happened."

He huffed. "The usual. I trusted the wrong person, and my team paid for it."

She didn't say anything but kept her hand in place. Compassion shone in her eyes.

"Back in my Army days, I was stationed in

Kabul . . ." Could he trust her with his story? Before he could second-guess himself, the words dislodged from his brain and spilled out all around them. "One day, we were pinned down with some insurgents in the area. My captain wasn't with us, so I had to make and execute the plans to get us out of there. We had a translator with us who helped us with the locals. He told us about a safe house we could use to get out of the danger zone."

A tremble rose through Grizz's body. He hoped Dani couldn't feel it. The smell of the acrid smoke hit him like it was right in front of him. The deafening explosion. The screams.

He swallowed. "It was a trap. The house was wired to blow. I trusted the translator, but he'd been working for the Taliban the whole time. My friend Kyle was the first to head to the house, based on my order. The whole place exploded the second he stepped on a trip plate at the front door. Two of my men were sent home with third-degree burns, but Kyle never made it home." Grizz's heartbeat raced. He'd never confessed this to anyone. "His death is on me."

"No." Dani's firm command startled him. "You don't get to hold responsibility for Kyle if Josh's death isn't my fault."

"I hear you. I need to take my own advice.

And I know that's true. Bad men did bad things, outside of my control. But there are things I can control—and who I trust is a big one. I've got my team, but I'm not letting my guard down with anyone else. I can't take that chance again."

Except his protective armor had started to show holes when it came to Dani. She'd made it through his perimeter checks, straight to his heart, and he hadn't seen her coming.

"Maybe it's time to let people in." Dani's blue eyes sparkled, and he refrained from reaching out to tuck a stray lock of hair behind her ear. "You can't shut people out to protect your heart. What if you miss the good stuff?"

The melody of his grandfather's favorite hymn stirred in his soul. "'Yes, when this flesh and heart shall fail, and mortal life shall cease: I shall possess, within the veil, a life of joy and peace.'"

Dani tilted her head. "That sounds kind of familiar. And it's true. We can't control life and death. But peace? That seems harder to come by."

"It's a verse from 'Amazing Grace.' My grandfather was always humming that song wherever he went. It kind of stuck with me."

Dani snuggled in closer, her head now resting on his shoulder. "But with that kind of peace, you'd have to trust God. That's not something that can be manufactured."

True. Maybe his grandfather's legacy was more than a cabin, more than a hideout in the woods.

Peace. Absolution for his misguided trust. Love.

Weren't those things the core of all human desires? To love and be loved. To trust unconditionally. Yet peace and love seemed like moving targets he'd never hit, even with the best longbow.

Grizz moved his arm and snuggled it around Dani. She turned, her face mere inches from his. His brain short-circuited from the nearness. She was the furthest thing from Candice. Strong. Determined. Fearless.

Beautiful.

He tilted his head, and she mirrored his movement. His lips brushed hers, and she didn't pull away. His mind shouted at him to stop, but his heart pumped out a different message. One he couldn't ignore.

Grizz ran a hand through her hair and broke the kiss. "What are we doing? You're going to head home, and I'm here. In the middle of Alaska."

She looked him in the eyes. "I think we're two people longing for connection. I don't know what might come of this, but I'm glad I've gotten the chance to meet you, Grizz. To see you in action with your team."

He stole another kiss, melting the loneliness away. She wrapped her arms around his neck and sank against his body.

The front door flung open, sending Dani and Grizz to separate ends of the couch in half a second.

Sanchez burst through the room. "Grizz! Kane is missing. Saxon and I have been looking for him, but there's no sign of him anywhere."

NINE

DANI WATCHED GRIZZ MORPH INTO an action hero right before her very eyes.

He grabbed the radio from the kitchen counter.

"Stay here, Dani. I'm going to go look for Kane." He raced out the back door with Sanchez.

The safe feeling of being in Grizz's arms eroded. If something had happened to Kane, it meant their hideout was compromised.

She sank into the plush sofa cushions and let out a long sigh.

Her mind replayed every second of that kiss—a moment she'd remember for the rest of her life. The man might look like a brute, but his kiss had been gentle, not demanding.

But he was right. What business did they have forming a relationship when they came from two totally different worlds?

Dani wasn't one for sitting idle in the midst of action. She walked to the sliding glass door that led to the wooden deck and peered out. The sunlight broke through the clouds and glinted off the water. She took a deep breath and enjoyed the view.

What would it look like if she had that kind of peace from the song Grizz had mentioned? If only she wasn't driven to always chase the next big thing.

Wait. Something moved in the woods to the right of the lake. It looked like a person. With a gray hotshot T-shirt.

Kane! He staggered closer to the tree line. Why had he been that far back in the woods? He stumbled and crashed to the ground. Didn't get up.

Dani raced to the kitchen. She needed the radio to let Grizz know she'd spotted Kane in the woods. The man was injured. But Sanchez and Grizz had headed out to the other side of the property to search. They'd taken the radio. And where was Saxon?

She needed to get help. Grizz's phone still

showed no bars. And without the radio, it would be impossible to get a message to him.

Dani's heart pounded. She needed to help Kane.

She slid the door open to the patio, took two steps outside, and a voice from behind her shot ice through her veins.

"Looks like we finally get to meet, INN reporter Dani Barlowe." A muscular arm snaked across her throat and pulled her into the shadows of the deck, against the wall of the house.

"Who are you?" Her voice rasped as the man flexed his forearm against her neck.

"I'm only going to ask one time. Where is the camera? We know you were there recording that night. Our security cameras caught you and that other snoop filming our hideout. If you give me the evidence, I won't hurt any of your new friends here. We'll leave."

Dani kicked and tried to scream, but he clamped a hand over her mouth. She gagged and choked.

She willed herself to stay calm, but the bitter taste of dirt from the man's hands made bile rise in her throat.

The man pulled out a gun and pushed the muzzle to her temple. "I see the hotshot I knocked out came to. I guess I should have just finished him off when I had the chance. But you're the prize. I've got no beef with the others. Just you and that big guy."

Had Grizz become collateral damage for helping her? The man tightened his grip around her neck.

"Where is the camera?"

"I—I don't have it. I gave it to someone else for safekeeping."

No sense in denying they had the evidence. But Grizz had the SIM card. It wasn't a lie. She didn't have the prize he sought.

Her vision blurred and she clawed at the arm pressed against her throat. She kicked and scratched, but lack of oxygen began to slow her reflexes.

The glass door to the deck slid open, and from the shadows, Dani watched Grizz walk out and inspect the area, his gun drawn.

She managed a squeak before the man slapped his hand over her mouth. Grizz's head spun in her direction.

"Hold it right there." The man dragged her across the deck. Her feet barely touched the ground with his beefy arm still wrapped around her neck. "Toss your weapon over to me."

"Jeremiah Redding. We meet at last." Grizz glared at the man. He leveled his gun at Jeremiah's head, but her captor shoved his weapon harder into her temple.

"Your girlfriend here says she doesn't have the camera. We know the reporters filmed us. Give me the evidence, and I'll let you walk away. Or I kill her in front of you. Your choice."

Dani struggled against him but couldn't catch her breath. Spots danced in front of her eyes. She couldn't hold out much longer.

"Looks like you have something I want, and I have something you want."

Grizz stood like a granite boulder, unmoving and unflinching. The anger sparking from his eyes could start a forest fire.

Where were Saxon and Sanchez? How could she end this standoff?

Grizz broke the tension. "I know where the camera is. But you're going to let her go."

"Nope. My orders are to keep her alive for some reason. It seems that someone has an obsession with the pretty reporter. But I don't care if she dies." He twisted the gun, and Dani couldn't stifle a whimper.

Think, Dani. Think!

God, I could use a rescue right about now.

The clouds parted in the sky, and her mind cleared. She knew exactly how they were going to get out of this mess.

She nodded her head as best as she could to get Grizz's attention. He shifted his eyes without moving his head.

Get ready, Grizz.

She felt around her jeans pocket for the knife Grizz had given her. She'd kept it on her, but she hadn't known what she'd do with it. Until now.

Minimizing her movements, she pulled the knife out and flicked it open. With what miniscule strength she had left after being deprived of oxygen, she drove the knife into Jeremiah's leg.

He howled and loosened his grip. Dani flung herself to the ground, wheezing and sucking in gulps of air.

The shot echoed cross the postcard-perfect Alaskan backdrop.

Jeremiah clutched his chest and stumbled backward, hitting the top step that led to the yard. He tumbled down the stairs, his eyes staring up at the sky, not blinking.

Grizz lifted her from the deck. "Don't look. You don't need to see another dead body."

But it was too late. She'd already seen the man's lifeless stare and the blood seeping from his chest.

The second the bullet had left his gun, Grizz had known Jeremiah wasn't going to make it.

He carried Dani into the house. Her bravery in the face of that horrible man warmed his heart. She was a fighter—his fighter—and he was going to do everything in his power to make sure she got off this mountain.

He put her on the couch and rearranged the pillows around her. Purple bruises were beginning to surface around her neck, but she seemed to be more stunned than injured.

The side doorbell chimed. Sanchez and Saxon were propping up Kane on either side. They set him down next to Dani on the couch.

Kane groaned. "I was ambushed. He conked me on the head and dragged me out into the woods. I tried to make my way to the house to warn you. Don't know where my radio went. Must have dropped it."

Sanchez returned from the kitchen with a bag of ice for Kane's head.

Dani touched her tender throat. "He—Jeremiah—told me his beef was with me and Grizz. That's why he didn't take you out, Kane. He came for the camera. They know we have the evidence to shut down their whole operation."

Grizz grimaced. Taking a life always took an emotional toll, even in self-defense. "Jeremiah won't be a threat any longer. I took him out on the deck."

Saxon looked at Grizz. "What do we do? This place is compromised. If you killed one of their men, they'll come for you even harder."

Grizz shook his head. "What is taking Rio so long to get here?"

"We've got to get that evidence to him." Sanchez paced, probably worried about Kane's injury, although she'd never admit it.

As if the moment had been scripted, the intercom chimed. Grizz raced to the wall panel that showed the activity at the main gate.

Rio's face filled the screen, and Grizz wanted to kiss the monitor. He hit the button to open the gate.

"Perfect timing. Rio is here. Now we can get this evidence into the right hands."

He had to get Dani out of this house and off the mountain before these lunatics realized Jeremiah had failed. This wasn't over, and these men would return—with reinforcements.

Sanchez opened the door, and Skye Parker

pushed her way through and had Dani pulled into a hug in a matter of seconds.

"Dani, you had me worried. And when Rio filled me in on what you discovered about the compound in the woods . . . I'm just glad Grizz found you."

Rio walked in behind Skye. "I brought reinforcements." Two other agents with FBI logos on their jackets followed Rio in.

"What happened here?" Skye said, looking from Kane to Dani.

"We had a run-in with Jeremiah Redding." Grizz took the camera's SIM card out of his pocket. "Here's the evidence from Dani and Josh's camera."

Rio crossed his arms and frowned. "Redding was here? And did that?" He pointed to Kane, who had a bag of ice covering his temple.

Grizz nodded. "Jeremiah jumped Kane, then snatched Dani. He held her at gunpoint, demanding the evidence. They apparently caught Dani on camera filming their compound. But Dani managed to stab him in the leg, and I shot him. He didn't survive."

Rio rubbed the stubble on his chin. The man looked like he hadn't slept in days. Rio nodded to the two agents, who headed out back. "I brought my laptop. I'm going to take a look at this SIM card. Dani, I'm so glad you're safe after your ordeal, but I'll have to take your statement once we get to base camp. Sorry to make you relive it, but your testimony is going to put these men away."

Dani moved into the kitchen, where Rio set up his laptop on the counter. "The camera captured a few faces," she explained. "It proves that Senator Geoff Deville was at the compound."

"Now that's interesting. With tangible proof of the senator's involvement, I can push the FBI to reopen the investigation. We'll get this guy."

Grizz stood behind Dani, his protective presence hard to miss. Even Rio shot him a side-eye of interest.

Rio turned to his screen and played the video. Dani turned into Grizz so she didn't have to watch, and he wrapped his arms around her. Rio muted his laptop so she didn't have to hear the fatal gunshot that had ended Josh's life.

"Dani, I'm so sorry you had to go through all of this." Rio closed his laptop and placed the device and SIM card in a briefcase that locked. "But we're going to take this group down, thanks to your bravery in getting this evidence. And if the senator is involved, we have the proof to lock him away. We'll run facial recognition to confirm that it was him, but to me, this evidence is airtight."

This might finally be over. Dani could return home and pick up the pieces of her life, with this ordeal becoming a distant memory. Except it also meant putting Grizz in her rearview mirror.

She shifted out of Grizz's embrace and turned to Rio. "I need to contact my boss. He'll need to be filled in on what happened. And he'll want me to report on this." She hesitated, her gaze bouncing between Grizz and Rio. "You can trust me not to impede the investigation. If I need to stay quiet about certain details, I will. I just want justice for Josh. But the station will want its story."

The reporter in Dani never quit trying to race to the top. Of course her station would want her to report the story—she was an eyewitness and an active participant in the events that had transpired on Copper Mountain.

Rio nodded. "I'll take care of notifying INN and your supervisor. But we've got to keep this under wraps. If the senator knows he's been compromised, he's going to pull out all the stops to keep you from talking."

"One interesting thing Jeremiah said was that someone wanted me alive," Dani said. "Could that be Deville?"

Rio grabbed his briefcase and walked toward the living room, where Skye and Sanchez were fawning over Kane. "That's a distinct possibility. But it could also be someone else we don't know about yet. For now, I think we need to get out of here. I don't trust that these men won't regroup and send reinforcements now that they know we're here. It's only a matter of time before they realize we killed one of their own."

Skye stood. "We have three cars. We'll leave one here for the agents and take the other two down the mountain. The roads are still pretty washed out, but we made it up here. We should be safe making our way to base camp. I've already radioed for a medic to meet us there. We've got to get Dani and Kane checked out."

Grizz helped Dani to the back of one of the SUVs and climbed in next to her. Rio jumped in the driver's seat and Skye in the passenger seat. The rest of the team rode in the second vehicle.

"At least now we're on paved roads," Grizz said, grabbing Dani's hand and giving it a squeeze. He didn't miss the look Rio shot him in the rearview mirror.

"Thanks. I'm just glad to have the evidence in safe hands." Dani turned her head to watch out the window.

Grizz watched the trees whip by as they descended Copper Mountain. Once Dani gave her testimony and the danger subsided, she'd head to DC. And he'd be here, setting up his cabin for winter.

Missing her.

His mind lingered on their kiss. It shouldn't have happened. He'd crossed lines, that solid double line, knowing the danger. It just made the inevitable that much harder.

He couldn't keep her, and he didn't belong in her world. Better to sever their emotional connection now rather than have some messy breakup down the road.

But for now, he'd relish the nearness.

Rio slammed on the brakes, and the car skidded to a stop on the isolated road. Dani and Grizz lurched forward, but the seatbelts kept them locked in place.

"What happened, Rio?" Grizz scanned the area, looking for whatever had spooked Rio.

"I saw something on top of that boulder." Rio pointed out the window to the granite wall hedging them in. "It looked like a glint of metal. We know these guys have a crazy amount of firepower. I—I just have a bad feeling we're being targeted."

Grizz opened his door. "I trust your gut. I

think we need to run for it." Grizz radioed the other car, and Saxon pulled in behind them and stopped.

A hiss sounded—an all too familiar sound. Grizz grabbed Dani's hand and pulled her into the trees beside the road. Rio, Skye, and the others from the second car all dashed into the woods.

Rio's car exploded in a fireball, just like the helicopter.

Another RPG.

TEN

THIS HAD TO END. ONCE AGAIN, DANI found herself running for her life through the forested mountain in Alaska, with gunmen tracking her every movement.

So much for peace. This was a nightmare she couldn't wake from. At least she had Grizz by her side.

Branches scraped her legs and arms. The heat from the blast still sizzled the air.

Grizz clutched Dani's hand and pulled her forward. "We'll be okay, Dani. We're going to split up from the others. I know my way to the base."

"These men must be stopped. I don't want to constantly be checking over my shoulder, wondering if this is the day the senator shows up."

Grizz maintained his fast pace. Dani's legs screamed for relief from the hills and exhaustion. But she refused to slow down. When was the last time she'd had any rest in the past two days?

"We're going to cut through the woods." Grizz's head swiveled, no doubt looking for signs of the gunmen ready to pick them off. "If we keep going down, we'll come to the part where the road doubles back. It's not much farther to the base from there."

"Where is the peace, Grizz? From the song. With all of the bad things in the world, how will we ever find it? I thought I had it. I prayed for God to rescue me from Jeremiah. And He did— He sent you. But now we're still being chased, and there's no end in sight."

Grizz slowed, giving Dani a chance to catch her breath. "When I saw that man with a gun to your head, I prayed too. And I have to believe things will work out in the end. But that requires trust . . . which you know isn't my strong suit."

His words rolled around in her head as she pushed forward. If Grizz could learn to trust, maybe she could let go of some of her need to be proven right.

If her career didn't pan out, what if her second chance involved a guy like Grizz?

A truck rumbled in the distance. Dani shrank behind a tree, ready to hide from the enemy. But Grizz kept hold of her arm.

"It's one of ours. Probably our team leader."

The truck stopped next to them. "Need a ride?"

Dani looked at Grizz to make sure it was safe.

"Perfect timing. Dani, this is my team leader, Mitch Bronson. We've made it to safety." Mitch didn't look like the average firefighter, with his dark-brown hair a tad too long and cowboy boots on his feet.

"Pleased to meet you." Dani took Mitch's hand as he helped her hop into the truck. "How did you know where to find us?"

"Communications were finally restored, and Kane radioed in that you needed some help. I sent another car to pick up the rest of the crew. They ran when they saw what had happened to your vehicle. But everyone is safe and accounted for."

Grizz jumped into the cabin of the truck and shot Dani a wide smile that sent her heart fluttering. Maybe it was leftover adrenaline lingering, because she refused to let her internal struggle win against her growing attraction to a rugged mountain man making her insides melt.

Dani squished in the middle, sandwiched between the two big guys. And she didn't mind one bit.

Another five minutes and they were back to where she'd started two days ago. The base camp where she'd first encountered Grumpy Grizz. But now she'd seen a different side of him. One she liked.

Skye and Rio were already at the base after Mitch's reinforcements had arrived to pick them up. Skye looped her arm around Dani's. "Come on, I'll show you around our home away from home."

Base camp didn't do this place justice. With a runway dividing the camp down the middle, the Midnight Sun base camp looked more like a winter lodge, complete with multiple cabins. Quonset huts and a mess hall dotted the right side of the runway, and what looked like office buildings and dormitories lined the left.

"This place is impressive."

Skye escorted Dani to the medic's office to get checked out. Aside from some bruises on her neck and throat, she was given the all clear.

"I'll finish the tour," Skye said. "I'll show you my quarters so you can clean up a bit."

The women's cabin had a common living and kitchen area surrounded by multiple rooms.

Skye offered Dani a change of clothes and let her freshen up before meeting Rio.

Dani and Skye walked toward the main office, a three-story building that would have fit in any city but contrasted with the Quonset huts and helipads of base camp. Modern yet rugged.

"I'll leave you here," Skye said. "I'm on duty tonight, and we're down a helicopter."

Skye left, and Dani turned around in the conference room. A long table with ten chairs divided the room. She walked to the window and stared at the snow-covered mountain peaks surrounding base camp. From her vantage point, she could see inside the airplane hangar and watched men and women checking their gear for the evening shift.

Where was Grizz? Would she be seeing him anytime soon? If only he could be with her during the interrogation . . . or rather *debriefing*. But she called them like she saw them.

Rio entered and handed Dani a hot cup of coffee, then motioned to an empty seat. "You look nervous. This is just a debrief. I need to hear your version of the story."

She sat. "I'm just not used to answering questions. I'm always doing the asking."

He took his laptop out and flipped it around it for Dani to view. "You faced some very dangerous men, Dani. And I'm impressed. Grizz told me you stabbed Jeremiah in the leg to free yourself. That's some pretty good survival instincts."

Normally she loved compliments, but the fact that Grizz had been bragging about her made her blush. "I'm not as girlie girl as I look."

He rotated the laptop back. "I never thought that of you. You've always struck me as strong and independent. And tenacious. Because of your footage, we have proof that the senator is involved with this militia group. I'm working on bringing him in for questioning. His days of evading the law are over. Not to mention you helped us stop Jeremiah Redding. He's been on the Most Wanted terrorist watch list for a number of years. Dani, this is good work."

Maybe her career could be salvaged after all. She had an eyewitness account of taking down a terrorist organization and a senator. Other networks would want to interview her.

Rio eyed her the way he probably interrogated a suspect, most likely operating out of habit. His dark eyes bored holes through her, causing her to raise her defenses to high alert. She definitely wasn't used to sitting on this side of the table.

Rio crossed his arms and stared at her. "You're morphing into reporter mode. I need to interview you as a witness to this crime. Can I trust you to keep everything we discuss confidential? We can talk about us possibly giving you the rights to the story, but I need your take on the events. Don't hold anything back."

"But you'll shut me out if you think I'm going to report on it."

"Dani, I've known you a long time. You and Skye are friends. And I know you'll do anything to take down this militia group and get these charges to stick to the senator. Can I trust you to keep this off the record? I'll let you know when you can release the official report."

Drat. Which was better—off-the-record information, or no information at all?

She mimed taking off a hat. "Look. I took off my reporter hat. All I want is justice for Josh. And if I get the story, that's a bonus for me. I told you earlier I wouldn't impede any investigation."

Rio relented on his laser-focused stare. Fine lines creased the corners of his eyes. "What I'm about to share is not for public consumption." He glanced around the room and leaned across the table. "We've confirmed that Sanchez's father was held prisoner at the compound in the woods. The group purchased him for his knowledge of biological weapons and delivery systems. They've kept him as a hostage, forcing him to work for the SOR."

Dani sipped her coffee. "That building with the smokestack is definitely concerning. It may be where they're creating or testing the weapons."

"That's what we're about to find out. I'm setting up a raid. Waiting on some reinforcements to arrive."

"Any way I can tag along? I'd love to see this camp destroyed for what they did to Josh. I want to be there when you take down every last one of these terrorists."

Rio's folding chair creaked as he leaned back. "I think your protector, Grizz, would have something to say if I brought his girl into the middle of a gunfight. These guys aren't going down easily."

"Grizz's girl? Oh please. He rescued me, and I'm eternally grateful, but that's the extent of our relationship. I need to be there."

Rio snorted. "You've got a target on you. These men have already proven they have their sights on you. I'm not even sure you're safe at the base. But I think it's better than you being out in the open."

Dani didn't like being sidelined. But before she could object, Mitch Bronson, Grizz's team leader, rushed into the room, followed by Sanchez.

"We just received a report of a fire. That compound in the woods is abandoned, and they're burning the place to the ground. Hotshots are going in."

Sanchez gasped. "What if my father is there?"

Bronson shook his head. "I don't think so. We got an arial view of the camp from the helicopter, and it looks like they've abandoned the place. It's empty."

Dani craned her neck to get a view of the action outside the window. Men and women raced to the vehicle compound, donning their gear. "Rio, let me go with them. My story has changed. I want to report on the hotshots in action. INN needs to make up for its bad press."

Grizz slammed the door to his room shut. He headed through the common area, grabbed his gear pack, and headed out the door.

He hadn't meant to eavesdrop, but when he'd turned the corner on the way to the conference room to find Rio, Dani's words had stopped him dead in his tracks.

That's the extent of our relationship.

And then she'd begged Rio to let her in on the compound takedown. So, this was how it ended.

Dani would get her story, while Grizz was left out in the cold.

At least he knew the truth of how she felt about him.

On his way to the vehicle compound, he almost ran Dani over. She stepped into his path, as if to block his way.

"I want to go with you." She stood in front of him, a defiant and fierce look etched into every facial feature. "I won't get in the way. I want to help. I need to be there when the hotshots save the day. I want to tell the story—"

He couldn't stifle the growl that erupted from deep inside. "That's all you do. Tell stories. Doesn't matter who you use." Had she used him? Had the kiss they'd shared just been her way to cozy up to him so she could get what she wanted?

"What does that mean?"

"Look, honey, I've got work to do, and you have a life to return to. Our commander, Tucker Newman, is heading to the airport to pick up some of Rio's team flying in for the investigation, and he offered to drop you off. We'll make sure you get your story. But you need to go back to where you belong. And that isn't here."

The fire in her eyes dissipated. His words had hit the intended mark. And just like that, he was the beast again. But it was for the best. "Go home. I've got work to do."

She took three steps back. "If that's what you want, Grizz. Go." She waved her hand to usher him forward. "I'm not stopping you."

He stomped to the vehicle compound. At least he knew it was over. There was zero chance of anything happening with Dani.

He knew she wouldn't stand up for their relationship, if it could even be called that. Sure, they'd had a few moments while they'd been on the run. However, their differences outweighed the few things they had in common. He was delusional if he thought for a second that he belonged in her world.

Grizz jumped in the back of the old school bus that transported the hotshots and their gear.

Kane gave Grizz a head nod. "This doesn't look good. The winds are shifting, and we need to contain the fire. Even with the recent rain, we don't want to risk any stray sparks igniting elsewhere."

Sanchez stared ahead. She was tough as nails, but knowing her father was still missing would break even the toughest hotshot.

Kane flanked Sanchez on the other side and gave her hand a squeeze. Grizz put a hand on Sanchez's arm. "We're going to find your father.

With Dani's evidence, we now know what we're up against."

Even if he'd just completely walked out on Dani, closing the door on any kind of relationship.

The bus bumped over the rocky dirt road. The big wheels hopefully would make it through the parts of the road that had washed out with the mudslide. But the driver would have to drive around the most direct path, looking for solid terrain.

Saxon nodded toward Grizz. "Take my mind off things, Grizz. What's up with you and the beauty queen?"

"Yeah," Kane chimed in. "I've never seen you so protective of anyone before." Kane's hand lingered on Sanchez's a little too long. Interesting, since he mocked Grizz's relationship status.

Grizz shook his head. "She only wants one thing. A story. I'm just a means to an end for her."

"I don't think so," Sanchez said. "Out of all of us, you saw a depth to her that we initially missed. She wants to avenge Josh's death and see my dad rescued. It's not a story anymore. She's invested."

Grizz snorted. "I can't believe she's fooled us all."

Sanchez stared at Grizz. "I've only spent a little

bit of time with her, but even I can see that she's not that self-centered. You have to let go and trust her to do the right thing. I think she'll surprise you in the end."

Was Sanchez right? This woman had been searching for her missing father, and now the man had disappeared again when she'd been so close.

Fearless. Just like Dani.

Grizz shook his head. He had to get Dani out of his mind for now. He had a fire to put out.

They saw the smoke billowing about a mile ahead. The truck stopped at the end of the washed-out road. Kane opened the door. "Looks like we're walking from here."

Grizz checked his radio to make sure it was in working order. He was thankful for a tech team that had worked around the clock to restore their communications. They grabbed their gear and hiked uphill.

Smoke wafted down the mountainside, and the roar and crackle of the fire grew louder with every step Grizz took. The smell of charred wood made his nose itch.

"Let's put this fire out." The order came from his team leader, Mitch Bronson, over their radio comms. "It looks like they were running more tests in this lab, so we can't assume we're deal-

ing with the same chemicals as at their last compound. Let's be careful."

Black puffs of smoke signaled their destination.

Grizz heard a gasp in the comms from Skye.
The smokejumpers had been dropped into the
area a few minutes before the hotshots. "What
a disaster. Parts of the complex have been decimated, and the fire is heading towards the main
building."

Despite the cool temperatures, sweat trickled
down Grizz's forehead.

A different voice interrupted the airwaves.

Rio.

"We just caught a break. We've received information that suggests the SOR has been testing
aerosol dispersal methods, maybe trying to find
the best delivery system. We may have destroyed
their warehouse, but I don't think we've seen the
last of this threat."

Could this day get any worse? Grizz remembered the fallout from before, with fish and animals dying after coming into contact with the
poison. If they released the same compound into
the air, the results could be devastating.

He refused to let his thoughts go there. He had
to focus on stopping the fire.

The dense trees cleared, and Grizz got a good

view of the compound from the same location Josh and Dani had snapped those pictures. Flames shot high into the sky from one building. But the main building remained untouched by the fire. So far. The fire was tracking toward the center—to the building where they suspected the chemicals were being housed. Grizz's anger raged hotter than the fire. If that building exploded, the chemical fallout could impact Alaska for miles.

For the second time today, Grizz prayed for a miracle.

ELEVEN

DANI PACED IN THE CONFERENCE room, unable to contain her nerves.

The compound was on fire, and with the complication of dangerous chemicals, the stakes were even higher. Dani heard the status updates through Rio's radio.

Grizz was prepared to enter a burning camp to stop the fire from spreading to that center building. She closed her eyes and could see the smokestack puffing out white smoke. She knew exactly which building housed the chemicals.

While she wanted to be part of the action, her stomach tightened at the thought of Grizz rushing into a burning building.

Her hero, whether he walked away from her or not.

A knock sounded at the door, and Rio looked up from his computer. "Jamie. I'm so glad you're here. We've got a lot of work to do."

A petite woman entered. Her cargo pants and boots made her look like she belonged in the Alaskan wild with Grizz. The two braids that hung over her shoulders made her look younger than she probably was, but her laptop bag and computer accessories communicated an air of authority.

"Jamie Winters is our tech wizard, and she's been following the money trail for quite some time on this case."

Jamie sat at the table and set up a complete workstation with two monitors and a printer. "Dani Barlowe. I've watched your newscasts. And I've heard how instrumental you were in getting us this intel."

Dani shot the woman a smile and took a seat across from her. While she knew the value of processing data and tracking the senator down, her mind was fixated on what was happening on Copper Mountain.

On Grizz and the rest of the hotshots.

Why had the radio gone silent?

Rio turned to her. "Look, I know you're worried about the fire on the mountain, Dani. But I asked Jamie to come in and debrief with you about the senator. We know he got off scot-free the last time he was indicted. We won't let him walk this time."

She sat back in her chair, her reporter instincts churning. "Where did these mercenaries get the money to create an elaborate high-tech secret base in the woods? A project that didn't catch the attention of local law enforcement or the FBI. They didn't spare any expense. An RPG took out a helicopter."

"True." Rio clicked away on his laptop keyboard, then looked up. "Jamie has been looking into the funding source. I just sent an email to have our forensic accountants look into any significant transfers of money from a key list of high-ranking government officials that we've had our eyes on. Let's see if this goes any higher than the senator."

Jamie turned her screen so Rio could read the information. "I've already been looking into Senator Geoff Deville's accounts. He's made several transfers that are all ten dollars under the limit that would draw our attention. To an offshore account."

Dani shook her head. "The senator was cleared of embezzlement. This doesn't definitively tie him to the funding of the terrorist group in the woods."

Jamie turned her laptop and made a few clicks. "Except these charges happened after his indictment. I think the whole thing was a cover-up. Sorry, Dani, but you were used. My hunch is he planted the fake story about the embezzlement, knowing there'd be an investigation. But he hadn't embezzled the money, at least not until a few months after he was cleared of all charges. Your story painted him as the victim, and he used the press to hide what he was really doing."

Rio sighed. "If the senator is funding the militant group with stolen money, he's probably bribing and threatening anyone who might be able to connect him to this. He's the one who quashed the investigation."

Dani said, "I've always suspected that he bribed that judge. Maybe my story wasn't that far off base."

The senator had used her to hide his crimes in plain sight.

The radio crackled and Grizz's voice rang through. "We're preparing to breach the building, but sparks have lit the main hut on fire."

"That's the place we suspect they're housing the chemicals." Dani fidgeted with her hair. Of course Grizz would be leading the charge to run into a burning building.

Everything within her wanted to be part of the action. Headlines began to spin in her mind.

Heroic Hotshots Race into Burning Building to Stop Deadly Chemical Fire. These men and women put their lives on the line to protect and serve the public.

This was the story she needed to share. Once she knew all the hotshots were safe.

She couldn't sit here any longer. "I need to use the restroom. I'll be back."

Dani headed down the hallway and found the bathroom. She splashed cold water on her face.

How could that slimeball Senator Deville somehow fund a terrorist camp in the woods? The same men who'd murdered Josh. The senator had questionable morals, but bankrolling killers? Clearly there was a master plan in the works.

But what was it? Why would the senator dabble in biological weapons? What was his endgame?

Water dripped from a faucet somewhere in the bathroom. Dani froze. Instinct told her she wasn't alone. Had Jamie followed her?

No, she would have seen the door open.

In the mirror, Dani saw a blur of black. A man in a mask hulked behind her.

She spun around but was too slow. An arm snaked out and grabbed her. A heavy hand clamped over her mouth.

A gloved hand covered by a white cloth.

She tried to bite down, but the grip held tight.

Her scream came out like a squeak.

She kicked and flailed her arms, but his hand shifted to clamp over her mouth and nose.

Air.

Her lungs burned.

His other arm squeezed her diaphragm. *Can't breathe.*

"You couldn't just leave it alone, could you? This is all your doing. But I've got plans for you."

The familiar voice jolted her, and she kicked harder. But the lack of oxygen began to take a toll.

"No! No." The rag muted her voice. The bitter taste of a chemical sealed her fate. Dani choked. The bathroom walls began to spin, and she lost feeling in her arms and legs.

With her last ounce of energy, she prayed. Not for herself.

But for Grizz.

The only way out of this mess for both of them was for God to perform a rescue mission.

Grizz knew they were out of time. Now that those embers had landed on the roof of the chemical plant, they had to move fast.

Get in. Stop the fire from spreading. Hightail it out of there. But without knowing what these men were up to in the compound, the dangers were unknown.

The hotshots headed into the compound and joined the smokejumpers at the edge of the camp. The thick smoke blinded Grizz, but he pressed forward, seeing only a few inches ahead of him with each step. He knew his team was marching directly behind him.

Grizz tapped his radio. "Sanchez, Kane, and I are going to check out the main door of the building to see what we're dealing with. Everyone else keep fighting the fires in the surrounding buildings. Watch the roof. We see a few hot spots."

The place was too quiet, and Grizz's stomach clenched. What were they walking into? One spark could ignite the chemicals and blast a crater in the side of the mountain. And with the winds this season, the last thing they needed was an explosion to rain toxic chemicals across the region.

He stopped at the steel door, an obvious sign of nefarious activity. Who put a thick, steel-reinforced door on a Quonset hut? Unless they were trying to keep people out.

Kane dropped his hose and hacked the handle and lock with his Pulaski. No luck. So he drove his axe through the metal siding in an attempt to create an opening for them to enter.

"Sanchez? Where are you?" Grizz looked around, but the smoke engulfed him like a curtain he couldn't see through.

"I'm right behind you."

Kane hammered until he formed an opening in the side of the building. Fire sizzled from the roof, and Grizz took an extinguisher off his back and plastered the area with foam.

He stuck his head through the wall to make sure there wasn't some gunman waiting for them in an ambush. The camp had been quiet, but he wasn't taking any chances.

Black smoke hung in the air, but the fire hadn't made its way inside. Yet. "Let's go."

Grizz moved a few feet into the structure. Rows of laboratory tables created aisles throughout the main area. One wall held empty bins.

Grizz pointed. "This is where they kept the weapons stash. I saw it in the recording."

"At your ten o'clock, Grizz." He turned to see what Sanchez indicated through the haze and took a few steps closer. Three white vats were arranged side by side against an interior wall, filled with liquid. Labels with a skull and crossbones warned them of the chemical cocktail behind the drums.

More tables held test tubes and lab equipment. This looked like a science experiment gone wrong.

Kane sprayed his hose at the ceiling, where the flames had melted a hole in the metal.

"Look out!" Grizz dove for Sanchez, knocking them both to the ground.

A blazing beam crashed to the ground—the very spot where they'd just been standing. Flames swirled around the roof of the building.

"Let's get that fire out," Grizz yelled into the radio. "It's getting dangerously close to the vat of chemicals against the north wall."

Water from the fire hoses rained down from the ceiling. Within a few seconds, the fire had dissipated into a hissing vapor.

"Good job, team." Grizz picked himself up off the dirt floor and extended his hand to Sanchez. "It looks like the fire is out inside. Keep watching the roof for more hot spots. We've got a lot of chemicals in here."

"Whoa." Kane's exclamation shot ice through Grizz's veins. "I found a body. Shot through the temple. Female in a lab coat."

Grizz heard Sanchez's gasp through the comms—probably thinking how that could have been her father. But who knew where they'd taken him now? Sanchez's search was starting from scratch.

Saxon began tearing through the walls of the building from the outside. Shouts came from outside as reinforcements arrived.

These men must have had several scientists working for them. But what were they making? He turned around the room in a circle, trying to figure out the endgame. Why all of the equipment and chemicals unless you were building something big?

There. In the back corner of the Quonset hut stood a metal rack. Grizz moved in for a closer inspection, and Kane followed.

"What is this?" Kane looked at Grizz, the concern evident on his soot-covered face.

"They look like canisters." Grizz studied the rows of containers. "Could this be their finished product? There's space for five."

"Yeah, but two are missing." Kane pointed at the two indentations where a canister would fit. But no canister.

"It's time to let the professionals figure that out," Grizz said. "Now that we know the fire is contained, we should get out of here. I don't like this place one bit."

The FBI would now secure the compound and examine the contents of the secret lab.

Kane, Sanchez, and Grizz headed out of the building through the hole Saxon had created.

The radio squawked.

"Grizz, is she there?" Rio's voice seemed strained.

Grizz looked around and responded. "Sanchez?"

"No. Dani. She headed for the restroom and never returned. I've been looking everywhere for her. I thought maybe she headed up the mountain."

Grizz's mind went numb. The radio fell out of his hand and hit the dirt. His legs wouldn't cooperate. He had to remind himself to breathe.

Dani was missing. And he'd never gotten to apologize for not trusting her. For walking away when she'd needed him most.

TWELVE

WHY WAS SHE SO COLD?

Where was Grizz?

Dani grasped around her, trying to find anything that could identify her location. But her arms were useless, tied up behind her back with zip ties while rope secured her to a wooden chair. The last thing she remembered was meeting with Rio. And someone else. Jamie?

They'd been discussing the senator's involvement in the terrorist organization.

Her mind opened a floodgate, and the deluge of memories assaulted her.

Grizz.

The mystery compound.

Senator Deville.

Assassin bugs.

She tried to move, but her stomach threatened to empty its contents all over the floor. She tried to feel around in her pockets, but her knife was gone.

No, no, no. Not good.

The man Dani had thought she'd ruined with her story happened to be exactly as she'd portrayed him. Evil.

How much time had she wasted feeling sorry for him—for herself? She'd been right all along, but that did little to comfort her when she was tied to a chair in an unknown location with a lunatic abductor. That man was as unstable as the fires Grizz and his team fought.

Fire! The compound was ablaze.

These militia guys were cleaning up. Which meant she was out of time.

Dani would be collateral damage. The senator wouldn't keep her alive for long.

She squinted to examine her prison cell. To her left, she spotted a rectangular window caked in dirt, but it gave her just enough light to make out some shapes in the shadows. She could see the outline of a door in front of her along with a few objects covered in sheets. In the corner, boxes were stacked against the wall. Storage? Maybe she was in a basement, based on the damp smell and dusty air.

"Hello?" A frail voice startled her.

"Who's here?" she said.

Something scuffed against the concrete floor. "I was going to ask the same of you. I'm Rodrigo Cortez."

"Cortez? I know your daughter, but she goes by Sanchez, not Cortez. She's been looking for you." She didn't want to say that the compound was currently burning to the ground. The man had been through a lot and didn't need to know his daughter was in danger.

He sucked in a breath. "My Maria has been looking for me? No. Please make her stop."

"What do you mean, Doctor Cortez?"

"Please, I don't want Maria involved. These men are very bad. They'll use her just like they're using me. She needs to stay far away."

Dani shivered, and not from the cold room. "What did they make you do?"

Another scraping sound. The man shuffled in what sounded like a chair scraping across concrete floor. She squinted in the dark and saw the silhouette of a rail-thin man with shaggy hair. He hopped the chair a few more spaces toward hers.

"They forced me to develop a bioweapon. They threatened my family. I had no choice."

Dani didn't want to voice the next question, but her reporter instincts were working overtime. "What kind of bioweapon?"

He sighed. "It's a toxin that attacks the nervous system—derived from nightshade. They plan to detonate the canisters over American farms in the Midwest, spraying the toxin and poisoning the crops and soil. America's breadbasket would be wiped out, leaving us to import the majority of our food."

Dani's heart thumped in her ears. Visions of bare grocery store aisles coupled with the skyrocketing price of staple goods filled her mind. Not to mention the United States' total dependence on other countries for basic needs.

Reporter mode pushed the fear out of Dani's mind. The more she discovered about this whole situation, the better their odds of stopping this terrorist attack from occurring.

Assuming she walked out of this alive to tell about it.

"How can we stop them?" Her throat tickled. What she wouldn't give for some water. "If you know everything about the devices, can you tell me if there's a way to deactivate them? We have to be able to stop this."

He inched even closer, keeping his eyes glued to the one door in the windowless room. Definitely a basement. But where?

In a whisper, he said, "I put a kill switch in the coding that renders the whole system inert when the code is entered. The canister and the delivery system will fall to the ground without exploding and can then be safely retrieved. You just need to—"

A noise silenced them both. Light flooded the room from the open door.

"Oh no you don't, Dani." The senator stood in a doorway. "Don't think for even a second that you have a chance to save the day. I hadn't expected you to wake up so soon."

Had the senator overheard Doctor Cortez's confession about a kill switch in the canisters?

There had to be a way for her to get this information to the good guys in time.

"I was just a pawn in your political game, Deville. I can't believe you let me take the fall for you." She *could* believe it but needed to keep the man talking. If he was as narcissistic as she suspected, maybe he'd reveal his endgame.

He scoffed. "That was all you. Every story you

put out just garnered more sympathy for me. I should thank you. But instead, I'm going to kill you and pin this whole compound in the woods on you. Maybe your FBI friends will find the special account you used to purchase a massive amount of chemicals. I can't help it if you're obsessed with me and want to ruin my life by making me look like the bad guy. But they'll be too busy looking for your body to come after me."

The man was seriously unhinged. Did he really think he could sidestep a conviction by making her take the fall for it? But based on the dark look in his eyes, he would kill her.

The senator kept one eye on his Rolex watch. "It's about time to leave."

A noise scuffed from upstairs. It sounded like footsteps. A man came into Dani's view, behind the senator.

"Finally. What took you so long?" The senator glared at the newcomer, a short man with dark hair. The guy clutched two silver suitcases and passed one to the senator, keeping a tight grip on the other.

Dani's mind spun to put the pieces together. The canisters. Could they be the bioweapons Cortez had talked about?

The senator nodded to the man. "We'll split

up. You take Cortez." Then Deville nodded at Dani. "I'm taking her."

The man cut the zip ties around Cortez's hands and feet and pulled him up by the arm. Cortez wobbled. The new guy gripped Cortez's upper arm and half pulled, half dragged him to the open door that led to a stairway.

Deville cut the rope to free Dani from the chair and yanked her up by the arm. Pain radiated from her shoulder to her fingers, but she refused to cry out.

She wouldn't show this man an ounce of fear.

He didn't cut the zip ties around her hands but shoved her forward. She worked hard not to trip.

"Where are we going?" she asked.

"Always the reporter. Asking way too many questions." With her hands behind her back, maintaining her balance was a challenge. Not to mention the lingering effects of chloroform.

Deville dragged her up some dimly lit stairs, through an opulent house, and into a kitchen. Her entire apartment in DC would fit in this kitchen.

He shoved her into a dining-room chair at a table built for serving fifteen people. "Sit and don't say anything."

She twisted her hands to see if she could get

out of the zip ties but wound up rubbing her skin raw. She checked out the kitchen island to see if there were any knives. If the senator turned his back, maybe she could grab something from the counter to cut the binds.

The picture window on the far wall of the kitchen overlooked the expansive backyard. A thrumming sound grew louder. Was that—a helicopter?

She watched out the window as the helicopter approached. It landed in a big white circle at the end of the lawn.

No. Dani wasn't getting on a helicopter with this man. Who knew where she'd wind up?

A scuffle in the hallway by the kitchen caught Dani's attention. Deville's lackey arrived and shoved Cortez into the chair across from Dani.

Deville moved to the table. "Our rides are here."

Rides as in plural? Dani's mind whirred at the implications. The men were going to separate so the cases wouldn't be together.

Which meant she and Cortez would probably be separated. But was she going to be leaving by helicopter?

The senator grabbed Dani from behind and

jammed the familiar white cloth over her mouth and nose. She struggled, but it was no use.

She was going to die, disappear without a trace, and no one would know she had her story.

And Grizz would never know that she'd loved him.

"Just breathe."

Rio's voice brought Grizz back to reality. His mind spun out of control. He'd hitched a ride on the helicopter and now sat in Mike's office.

But his thoughts could only focus on one thing.

Dani.

Grizz stood and paced the six-by-ten office. "Where is she? We will find her."

Rio leaned on the doorframe with his arms folded. "Senator Deville is our top suspect, and he has that mansion on the other side of the mountain. Jamie uncovered the property in his second wife's name. She also pieced together the money trail that will be the final nail in his coffin when we arrest him. If Dani isn't there, he might have left something behind that could tell us where she is. I'm getting a SWAT team in place to raid the house."

"Not good enough. I have to be there for her. I can't let it end this way." Still in uniform, Grizz could smell the smoke that clung to his shirt. But he wasn't going to clean up. He wasn't going anywhere until there was a plan in place to rescue Dani.

The woman Grizz loved. "Rio, you have to let me go. What if the team doesn't get there in time?"

Rio looked over his shoulder to see if anyone might overhear his next statement. "Tucker is letting us *borrow* the helicopter if we promise to not let it get blown up like the last one. I've got a pilot that can get us near the property, and we'll take a few agents. I don't want him to get away." He pointed at Grizz. "You're not a trained FBI agent. Your job is to observe and be there for Dani. Tell me you understand."

"I understand." It didn't matter. Grizz would say anything to get one step closer to finding Dani. If he got his hands on the senator . . . Maybe it was a good thing Grizz was just *observing*.

He might not have always done the right thing, but he'd get there in time to save Dani. But he couldn't do it alone, not in his own strength. It was time to step up and be the hero he knew he could be—because of the strength God had given him.

You were right, Grandpa.

The tune to "Amazing Grace" filtered through his mind. *Yes, when this flesh and heart may fail, and mortal life shall cease: I shall possess, within the veil, a life of joy and peace.*

Dani had prayed, and he'd arrived just in time to stop Jeremiah.

Lord, please let this be a successful rescue operation coordinated by You. I can't do this alone. I trust You with Dani's safety.

Grizz stopped at his quarters and filled his lightweight backpack with supplies, grabbing his backup knife and some zip ties—anything and everything he might possibly need—before heading to the helipad. He was walking into this situation blind.

The ride took twenty minutes, which was nineteen and a half minutes too long for Grizz.

And once Dani was safe, he was never going to let her go. She made him want to be a better man. Less grumpy. He'd been hooked from the moment she'd called him her hero. Even if it meant that he lost everything to be by her side. He'd do it.

For her.

The helicopter landed down the road from the house. Grizz trudged behind the SWAT team, keeping an eye on his surroundings for any signs of trouble.

They walked the winding driveway to the house, officers in the lead with guns drawn. If Grizz thought Mike's cabin was a bit on the pretentious side, the senator's estate was ten times more so. From the air, the house looked like it had two swimming pools in the expansive and well-manicured yard. Not to mention the ornate lawn complete with marble statues.

Grizz felt for his sidearm on his hip. A motor roared to life. The familiar flap-flap-flap of helicopter blades whirred.

No! Not good. If the senator had a helicopter, the man could flee with Dani and they'd struggle to follow. They could chase with their helicopter, but it would take time to rally and get to the helo. The senator would be long gone.

Two officers slammed the front door with a battering ram while two others crept around the side of the house toward the back. Would they be too late?

"Outside. Stop that helicopter." Rio shouted orders into the radio and ran into the house.

Grizz raced through the front hallway just in

time to watch through the kitchen window as the helicopter rose and became smaller and smaller as it drifted toward the mountain peaks.

They'd never catch it. Dani was gone.

Rage seeped out of every pore. Grizz stomped through the house and out the front door.

He might never see Dani again. Never hold her. Never tell her his true feelings.

"Why, God? Why would you bring her into my life just to take her away? I trusted you. I—I still do. Please. Make a way."

Another noise from the opposite side of the house caught Grizz's attention. One of the doors in the three-car garage lifted.

A Rolls Royce pulled out of the garage and headed down the driveway.

Grizz radioed Rio. "A car just pulled out of the driveway."

But only static answered.

Great. What if Dani was in that car? Or maybe Sanchez's father.

He had to go after it. Grizz raced to the garage and dove under the door as it was about to close. Hopefully the driver hadn't been looking in the rearview mirror. The place had a multitude of options, but Grizz found a motorcycle parked in the far corner of the garage. He pulled the bike out and walked it around the other sports cars.

The keys dangled from the ignition. Grizz hit the button on the panel for the garage door, jumped on the bike, threw on the helmet, and took off after the car, praying for his fifth miracle this week. "Please let me find Dani."

The mountain road wound, but Grizz never let up on the throttle. Whoever was driving couldn't have gotten far. The bike would have an easier time navigating than the car.

The hills rushed by him, and all of his childhood days riding dirt bikes came back to him. Sure, this bike was bigger and fancier than his dirt bikes, but he knew how to navigate those hairpin turns.

There!

Rounding the bend in the road, Grizz saw the vehicle. He'd been down this way before when visiting Mike. There was a switchback up ahead. Grizz could ride through the terrain and cut this guy off.

He raced through the dirt, leaves, and rocks. Dodged tree branches and bushes. Slowed in a few spots to make sure he didn't spin out his tires. But ahead, he saw the edge of the road. He parked his bike and ducked behind a tree, his gun ready.

The car approached, slowing as it neared the turn. Grizz took aim, and with one bullet, blew out the driver's side tire. The car fishtailed, and Grizz managed to get off another shot, taking out the back left tire.

The car shuddered to a stop on the shoulder. A man opened the driver's door, sticking his gun out first.

There was no mistaking the senator. Deville ducked behind the car door, using it as a shield.

Grizz stood behind his tree, never moving, gun trained on Deville.

The man tried to make a run for it, heading to the rear of the car. Grizz sent a shot that sliced through Deville's shoulder. The man screamed and fell to the asphalt.

Deville fired his gun, but the shot went wild. Grizz approached him from behind and stepped on his wrist until Deville loosened his grip on the weapon. Grizz kicked the gun out of the man's reach and pulled the zip ties out of his backpack, thankful he'd stopped to grab a few supplies earlier. He secured the senator to the door handle. Blood dripped down the designer suit from the wound in his shoulder.

"It's over Deville. Where is Dani?"

"I don't know what you're talking about. You

don't know who you're dealing with. When I'm through with you . . ."

Grizz walked away and headed to the end of the car. He tapped on the trunk, and someone knocked back.

Dani!

Grizz rushed to the front seat and grabbed the keys from the ignition. He clicked the button for the trunk and popped it open.

Dani lay on the floor of the trunk, gagged and tied up but very much alive. He pulled the gag from her mouth.

"Grizz. I knew you'd rescue me." Her words were slurred. It looked like the senator had drugged her.

He lifted Dani out of the trunk, cradling her in his arms. "You're safe now. And I'm never letting you go."

THIRTEEN

ALMOST DIDN'T MAKE IT." DANI STOOD in the driveway of the senator's house, giving Rio a play-by-play of how Grizz had saved her life.

Once Grizz had freed her from the trunk, he'd radioed for backup. Officers had picked up the senator, and Grizz had given Dani a ride to the mansion on the motorcycle.

Dani had also brought the case with the canister and handed it to Rio, who had been busy trying to track down the fleeing helicopter.

Grizz handed the keys to the bike to Rio. "It's a nice bike."

Rio snorted. "I love your definition of the word *observe*. But you apprehended the senator. I owe you one."

Grizz had saved not only the day but her life. Again. But did he want her to stick around?

Rio squinted in the sun—the first sunny day Dani had seen since arriving in Alaska. Had it only been three short days ago?

So much had transpired. Her brain fog began to lift.

She gripped Grizz's arm. "The other canister. Cortez. Kill switch . . ."

"Slow down, Dani." Rio passed the case off to two other officers. "Just take a deep breath. What did you learn about the canisters?"

She took his advice and inhaled. "They were making biological weapons in the compound. They have five in total. The senator took one of the suitcases, and a different man—the one who took Cortez—had the other."

"This tracks with what I found at their compound. We found containers with spots for five canisters. But there were only three on site."

"So, we now have one biological weapon unaccounted for along with a missing scientist." Rio ran his hand through his hair. "Local police found the senator's helicopter abandoned on the other side of Copper Mountain. They're still searching for the suspect and Cortez."

Dani said, "I saw Sanchez's father. He told me

their entire plan. They want to poison our food supply via airborne dispersal of a neurotoxin. But Cortez put a kill switch on the devices. We just need to find the missing one before anyone else gets hurt." Memories of Josh flitted through her mind. These men had caused enough death and destruction.

Rio barked more orders into a cell phone while he wrote notes on a notepad and talked to them. "We'll get Doctor Cortez back, and that device. They're not getting away." He ran off as fast as he'd approached.

A car pulled up in the driveway. Kane and Sanchez. Dani let go of Grizz's hand and raced up to Sanchez. The woman had an expectant look in her eyes.

Dani took the woman—who clearly wasn't a hugger—and wrapped her in a bear hug. "Your father is alive. I spoke with him."

Sanchez softened in Dani's embrace. "Thank you."

"He was taken on the helicopter, but the FBI will find him. He's too valuable for these men to hurt him." But even still, the older man hadn't looked to be in good health.

How much longer would he last?

Sanchez took a step back. "Thank you, Dani. And I'm so glad you weren't hurt."

Dani shivered. The senator could have killed her. The same way she'd been inches from death so many times since she'd arrived in Alaska.

God had done the impossible. He'd sent Grizz.

If her hero hadn't gotten there when he had—

A helicopter landed with more FBI agents. Radios squawked and a local news crew pulled up on ATVs, their network windbreakers flapping in the mountain breeze. People raced around her, on a mission. After all, there was still one container of a biological weapon unaccounted for.

But she couldn't shake the daze. Because despite the continued threat to national security, her job here was done. She'd leave Alaska and go home.

Except a little piece of her didn't want to leave.

Grizz walked up to her as she stood by the tree line, taking in all the action. She should be the one reporting this. Not that she was in any shape to be on camera. Blood caked her wrists from the zip ties Deville had used. Her hair was matted, and she had another hole in her shirt.

She sighed. Grizz looked at her. "What is it?"

"These boots *are* ridiculous. What was I thinking?"

"I think your boots are a perfect reflection of you. They survived. They've been dragged through the mud, and you are still on your feet. Those boots are resilient and don't know when to quit."

"You're right. I don't know when to quit." She sighed. "And I'm not giving up on us. You're not getting rid of me that eas—"

His lips met hers, cutting her off mid word and silencing her mind. Warmth chased the Alaskan chill away. She sank into his kiss, wrapping her arms around his neck, pulling him closer to her. His beard tickled her chin, but man, could this guy kiss. His fingers tangled in her hair.

She might be going home to DC, but her heart had made a home here in Alaska.

With this man.

He moved back an inch, his muscular arms still wrapped around her. "I'm so sorry I walked out on you. I know your heart. You're more than just a story. The truth is, I just thought that I couldn't compete with your fancy DC life."

"You don't have to compete. I thought I knew what I wanted. But I was wrong."

"So, don't you want to be out with the reporters? This story is yours. You lived it—earned it. You should be the one to break it to the world.

If it wasn't for you coming up here to investigate after the FBI's hands were tied, who knows how much worse things might have been?"

She leaned up and kissed Grizz again. He tasted like dirt and salt, but she didn't care. They'd been through the wringer together, and that dirt streak across his forehead was a badge of honor. One that she wore too.

She took a step back and placed her hands on his chest. "Maybe it's time I tell a different kind of story. One about the hero hotshots who rescued me and saved the day."

"Ah-hem." They hadn't noticed Rio approach them. "Sorry to interrupt, but—" He pointed to a group of cameras perched at the edge of the driveway. Instead of pointing at the senator's house, the evening news would now have Dani and Grizz's kiss playing on an endless loop.

"Oops." Dani should feel embarrassed, but there was something about the Alaskan air that made her not care. Or maybe it was the person she was with.

Rio looked like he was about to smile as he stared at them. "Well, I need to borrow Grizz to get his statement."

Grizz kissed her hand and let it go. "I'll meet you at base camp."

Dani couldn't take her eyes off the man as he ran toward Kane and Sanchez. She and Rio walked toward the line of reporters. One man broke rank and charged her way.

Her boss. James Smythe.

She smoothed her hair down with her hands. How had he gotten here so fast?

"I came as soon as the FBI called to let me know about Josh." They let a silent nod of understanding pass between them. "The police have recovered Josh's remains," James said. "The family is planning a service in a week."

And then, just like that, she was back to work. Investigative reporter Dani Barlowe for International News Network.

"I've got you an exclusive INN interview first, where you'll get to tell about how you not only uncovered a terrorist plot but also escaped capture and survived the wilds of Alaska. Throw in a bear story or two. The viewers are going to love you. And that lumberjack you were making out with. Disgraced reporter heads to Alaska to clear her name only to uncover a deadly terrorist plot funded by Senator Deville. But the bigger story is, did you find love while running from gunmen? This story sells itself. I can't wait to put you on a press junket, giving your eyewitness interview to all the news outlets. How fast can you get to DC? Will your new boyfriend give us an exclusive interview?"

James's rapid-fire statements made Dani's head spin. Or maybe it was the chloroform still wearing off.

She looked around while James prattled on about a publicity tour. Cameras lined up on the senator's lawn, jockeying for the best position. A news helicopter hovered nearby. This political circus used to fuel her, give her a sense of purpose.

But now it all seemed so empty. Lonely.

It was as if life were handing her two mutually exclusive options for her future. Career or love.

She'd be forced to make that choice. And her career might not take first place.

Grizz wasn't going to let Dani walk out of his life without him letting her know how he felt about her.

If only he could get a few seconds of her time. They'd headed back to base camp, where she'd been whisked away and transformed from lost-in-the-woods to professional newscaster in the blink of an eye. When had she had time to change?

Now he was stuck in another meeting with Rio. His third debriefing.

"I just wanted to read you in on a few things." Rio sat at the conference room table across from Grizz. "We're holding a press conference in about an hour. Dani will tell her version of the events."

Grizz squinted. "But the investigation isn't over. We've still got a missing biological weapon. And Doctor Cortez—"

Rio raised his hand. "I know. Trust me. We've looked at the situation from every angle. But the FBI is going to 'close the case.'" Rio made air quotes around *close the case*. "The senator is behind bars where he belongs. The canister was recovered. If we unofficially close the case, the perpetrators will think they've gotten away with it. And that's going to work to our advantage."

"So you want me to corroborate the case-closed story."

"Yep. You're sworn to secrecy. We're investigating, but as far as the world knows, we've got our man."

Rio talked about the press conference, but Grizz caught sight of a blue wisp passing by the conference room door.

Dani. In that blue floral dress from earlier, complete with high heels. He wanted to bolt out the door after her, but Rio was still talking. Or wait, when had Rio stopped talking?

The man shook his head. "You've got it bad for Dani."

Grizz shrugged. No use hiding it. Rio knew him too well. "I need to find time to talk with her before she heads home. Look, I don't know what's going to happen, but I'm willing to make changes to have her in my life. This isn't the end."

Rio's smile widened. "Well, we need to make sure you find her right after the press conference. I know she's leaving tonight. Her station is making appointments for interviews across the country."

Rio and Grizz made their way across base camp to the hangar where the press conference would be held. Base camp had become a hotbed of activity. FBI, reporters, and military personnel littered the area.

The hanger had been converted into a mini conference room complete with a stage and microphone stand. A few of the hotshots and smokejumpers pitched in and set up chairs. Reporters lined up their cameras, and the generators hummed while working overtime.

Grizz surveyed the room. No sign of Dani. People started to fill the seats, and Rio and Grizz staked some chairs out in the last row.

"Are you ready for the circus to begin?" Rio asked.

"At least I'm not in the hot seat. Apparently, the media is clamoring for an interview with me, but so far I've dodged them all."

"I'm surprised you haven't headed out yet, gone to hide in your cabin. Away from the lights and cameras."

Grizz shrugged. "Not without seeing Dani first. We haven't talked about our relationship, if there is one."

Rio slapped Grizz on the back. "The world saw that kiss earlier. There's definitely a relationship. You just have to work out a few kinks."

"Like the three-and-a-half-thousand-mile distance, plus four time zones?"

"I have a good feeling about you two kids."

The volume of chatter grew louder as more people filed into the hangar. Dani was scheduled to give her story and answer questions. Would his name come up?

She entered the hangar with two other reporters from INN, and they walked to the makeshift podium his team had moved from their briefing room.

A man, Dani's boss, stood behind the microphone.

"Thank you for coming. While we mourn the loss of our colleague Josh Whitlock, we are thankful for the safe return of Dani Barlowe. We set up this press conference before Dani leaves Alaska and heads to DC as an opportunity for reporters to ask her questions about her harrowing journey. However, her flight has changed, and she'll need to head to the airport in one hour, so we're going to keep this brief."

Could this guy be any more dramatic? Probably. But Grizz focused on his words *leaving Alaska* and *one hour.*

How could he sum up his feelings for Dani in an hour and get five minutes of her attention?

Kane and Sanchez filled the remaining seats near Grizz, while Saxon stood behind Grizz, leaning against the back wall. All eyes were on Dani.

She rolled with the questions like a true pro.

Were you scared being out in the wild with terrorists chasing you?

Tell us about your confidential source.

What was it like being held captive by the senator?

What happened in the woods the night Josh Whitlock was murdered?

But no mention of Grizz or the weapons. Dani must have agreed to the press conference as long as no one brought up her kiss with Grizz. And the FBI had quashed the biological weapon story to let the bad guys think they were winning.

A few more questions referred to Dani's past with the senator.

Dani had perfectly tailored responses to all questions. Except one.

A reporter stood when called on. "What's next for your career, Dani?"

She looked right at Grizz, her blue eyes sparkling with amusement. "That depends. I have a lot of options on the table, and I'll take some time to review them."

The reporter with BBC on his hat scratched his forehead at the vague answer. But before the man could follow up, Grizz stood and raised his hand.

She nodded to Grizz that he had the floor. At an internationally televised press conference. Rio reaffirmed him with a nod and a smile.

He cleared his throat. What was he doing? A quick prayer and he opened his mouth, not knowing what was going to come out. "Is there any scenario on the table where you'd stay in Alaska?"

Everyone in the room turned to Grizz in unison, but he locked his eyes on Dani's.

Her smile lit up the room more than the flashes

from the cameras snapping pictures. Was he grinning like a fool?

"I think the answer depends, Mr. Grizz. What reasons would I have for staying here?"

A hush fell over the room, all eyes glued to Grizz. But all he saw was Dani and a future with her.

"Love."

Gasps followed by silence as all heads swiveled to Dani.

"While love is noble, I find it hard to commit to a man when I don't even know his first name." She giggled, and the attention shifted back to him like spectators watching a ball at a tennis match.

Was she really going to make him reveal his biggest secret to the world? No one knew his first name.

No one.

Until now.

He gritted his teeth. "It's Melvin. Melvin Grizz."

The room erupted in laughter, chatter, and flashes from cameras capturing every second of the moment.

Dani interrupted the chaos. "I'd like to readdress the question the BBC reporter asked regarding my future plans. I would like to announce my retirement from INN. I will be staying in Alaska. Indefinitely. I plan to work on my own independent documentary to introduce the world to the true Alaskan heroes. The hotshots."

Applause deafened the space, but everything faded around Grizz. Several friends slapped him on the back and called him Melvin.

The press conference ended, and Dani made her way to Grizz, passing the throngs of people wanting to talk to her. Her boss looked ticked. Her competitors high-fived her.

Grizz closed the gap between them until they were a few inches away from each other. "I'm all in, Dani. I love you. I might still be a bear at times, but I'm never going to walk away from you again."

She wrapped her arms around his neck and pulled him down for a kiss that made his toes curl. He didn't even care about the whistles a few of the hotshots made. This moment was about him and Dani. And their future together.

"I love you, Grizz. And don't worry, I'll never call you by your first name. Your secret is safe with me."

BONUS EPILOGUE

Thank you for reading *Burning Truth*. We hope you loved this story. Find out what happens next for Dani and Grizz with a **Bonus Epilogue**, a special gift, available only to our newsletter subscribers.

This Bonus Epilogue will not be released on any retailer platform, so get your free gift by scanning the QR code below. By scanning, you acknowledge you are becoming a subscriber to the newsletters of Kelly Underwood, Lisa Phillips, and Sunrise Publishing. Unsubscribe at any time.

THANK YOU

Thank you so much for reading *Burning Truth*. We hope you enjoyed the story. If you did, would you be willing to do us a favor and leave a review? It doesn't have to be long- just a few words to help other readers know what they're getting. (But no spoilers! We don't want to wreck the fun!) Thank you again for reading!

We'd love to hear from you—not only about this story, but about any characters or stories you'd like to read in the future.

Contact us at www.sunrisepublishing.com/contact.

READ ON FOR MORE FROM

CHASING FIRE:
ALASKA

Gear up for the next Chasing Fire: Alaska
romantic suspense thriller,
Burning Justice by Lisa Phillips

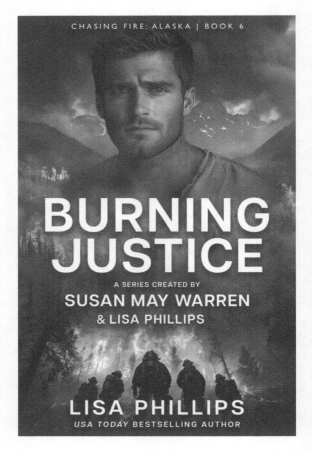

RESCUE. DANGER. DEVOTION. THIS TIME, THEIR HEARTS ARE ON THE LINE.

She's been searching for her father for fifteen years...

Maria Sanchez has spent her entire career as a CIA operative searching for her father, and she's not going to let some tough, arrogant former-soldier-turned-hotshot stand in her way.

His life was upended on a single fateful mission...

After being betrayed, branded a traitor, and declared dead, Kane Foster has a lot prove—and he's not going to let his team—or his country—down. Even if he has to douse the sparks between him and his feisty teammate. Because some things are more important than love.

Now someone tell that to his heart...

As the smoke clears on this pulse-pounding series, buried truths will be uncovered and loyalties tested in this sizzling finale to the Chasing Fire: Alaska romantic suspense series.

ONE

ALMOST A DECADE AS A SPY FOR the CIA hadn't prepared Maria Sanchez one bit for this life. Fighting wildfires in the Alaskan backcountry. Trying to stop a dangerous militia group from deploying a biological weapon on US soil.

Okay, so that last one was a bit more her speed.

Still, talk about being unprepared.

Kind of like the way she felt every time *he* looked at her. Kane Foster. Broody. Quiet. A former soldier, a guy who put loyalty above everything.

Cue heart fluttering.

Until the rumble of thunder split the sky, growing like a wave until it crested right on top of them. It sounded so close that Maria ducked, tucking her knees up to her chest and holding on tight. The way her father had always told her to. She tipped her head back against the mossy tree to watch the sky light up over Denali Mountain.

"There you are."

She flinched and turned to look over her shoulder but didn't uncurl her limbs. The night air had a chill.

"Need my sweater?" Kane reached for his zipper. Dark-blond hair, short on the sides but with the top sticking out all over because he didn't care to fix it. Stubble across his chin because he didn't care about that either. But the man cleaned up good on a Friday night, that was for sure.

She shook her head. The point was to *not* need anything, because needing things from people never ended well.

He settled beside her on the ground, close enough that she could feel his warmth. "Impressive storm."

She turned back to the sky stretched out in front of them. Above them. "This was a good place to stop for the night."

Kane nudged her elbow. "That means you're supposed to be getting some sleep, like everyone else."

"I signed up to take watch. Keep an eye on the fire."

"Right." His low chuckle drifted over. "That's why you're hiding over here, pretending you're alone in the dark."

"It's not as impressive if you feel safe. Storms are supposed to be dangerous and out of control. You're supposed to be a little afraid."

"Don't worry, I am."

Maria didn't think he was talking about the weather—or wildland firefighting. They'd been doing that for two seasons now. Laying low. Pretending they were regular folks who wanted a career change. Anything other than what they actually were.

Or why they were out here.

"Fear is a tool." Lightning cracked across the sky, making her pause before she continued. "It keeps you sharp. If you don't learn how to control it, you'll get swallowed up."

The storm whipped up some wind, blowing through the valley below and ruffling her hair across her face. The ever-present tang of burnt wood hung on the breeze. An odd, discordant presence that reminded her every second that the fire on the horizon was destroying property and vegetation, growing. Moving. Flames that seemed to flicker with life, trying to devour everything in its path.

She slid the dark strands that had come loose from her ponytail behind her ear. How well she knew fire, and the knowledge she had should be an asset and not a liability here.

After everything she'd been through, there had to be good. All the team members who studied the Bible now, talking about God working all things for good.

Whatever Kane thought about what she'd said about fear, he didn't share with her. He sat quietly, hopefully enjoying the night now that the sun had finally set. In three or four hours, it would rise again.

Of course she was going to sit out here trying to figure out how to solve all this.

"I thought about giving up, you know." Talk about fear. She barely even wanted to admit it. "He's been gone nearly fifteen years. I wondered if he wanted to be gone. If he chose to stay away."

"Now you know that was never true."

"But I believed it." She winced. "I would've quit because I lost the faith that I would ever find him. That I would get my father back."

A couple of weeks ago, a reporter had seen her father being held at gunpoint. Maria was closer to finding her father now than she'd been in fifteen years.

"I feel like every time we get somewhere with the search, we immediately get knocked back three steps." She ducked her head, ashamed to say she was losing the strength to fight. "We can't keep chasing him forever and live our lives. By the time we find him, he's gone. Moved on."

Kane nudged her elbow with his. "We didn't get this close only to lose him now."

"You said that in Montana, and he was gone before we found where they were keeping him." Maria turned to look at him and realized his face was closer than she'd thought. In the dark, she could barely make out his features.

But she didn't need the light to know what he looked like. She'd spent nearly two years with this man. His green eyes. His furrowed brow and crossed arms when he needed to think in silence. The two-day stubble across his jaw. His broad shoulders that made her want to curl up in his arms and let him impart some of that strength to her.

"I have to find him," Maria said. "Before it costs me the rest of my life."

Kane cleared his throat. "None of us is going

to quit. You're not fighting alone. We all agreed to do this together."

"Right." The team.

The Trouble Boys. Hammer, Saxon, and Kane. Members of the same Delta Force unit. Brothers who had fought and bled—and been declared dead—side by side. And Hammer's little brother, Mack. The kid no one wanted to leave behind.

Her protectors. Her family.

Kane tossed a small stone a few feet away. "You should get some sleep. I'll take watch. It's going to be a long day tomorrow if we're gonna quash this fire before it can jump the highway."

"You're right."

He stood and held out his hand. She reached up and grabbed his wrist where he had the tattoo of his unit under a leather cuff. Let him pull her to her feet. They both let go like a spark of static electricity had hit them. But it never did—because they didn't allow it to go that far. Hammer had made it clear that getting distracted and exposing themselves could cost them all a future. Fighting wildfires was a great way to stay off the grid while they continued their search for Doctor Cortez and the man who'd betrayed them.

First following leads in Montana.

Now up here in Alaska.

Since their team had been declared killed in action on the same day they'd rescued Maria from captivity in Syria, they'd been trying to get their lives back. It hadn't taken long to realize doing so wouldn't be all that easy—namely because they'd been attacked almost immediately after leaving and Kane had been captured.

They'd barely made it out of Syria alive, but they'd learned something important.

Someone powerful didn't want them to see the light of day.

At that point, they hadn't even known about the plan in the works, the threat to the country that they knew now they had to stop. All they'd known was that they had to lay low long enough to figure out what had happened.

Back then it had been about finding the man who'd betrayed them. Who'd held Maria, and then Kane, and cost them all their lives.

After they'd gone looking for answers and discovered her father's name on a stolen report, they'd quickly realized it was also about finding Doctor Cortez. The fact she and Kane had been nursing these feelings for each other had nothing to do with the mission parameters. Giving in was a temptation that didn't help them reach their goals—a distraction that could cost them the future.

Now that they knew it was all connected, the guys were as invested in this plan to set everything back to rights as she was. Joining forces with them meant she had to not jeopardize their chance to restore their reputations and get their lives back.

She walked by him. "Good night, Kane."

"Good night, Sanchez."

Another peal of thunder rumbled across the sky. As much as she wanted to pretend she was alone, just her and nature in all its destructive power, she hadn't been alone for a while now. She might have lost a lot, but what she'd gained were men who would risk everything to help her. Who believed as she did that the world was worth saving and that good people should be able to live in peace and safety.

Maria picked her way between the trees, over to the spot where the rest of the hotshots had chosen to make camp for the night. Basic bedrolls had been laid out, packs for pillows. She spotted the outlines of her boys and the empty spot for Kane. Hammer lifted his head as she passed, so Maria signaled with a handwave that everything was fine.

She passed the spots where Mitch—their hotshot crew chief—and Grizz lay a few feet from each other. Grizz had an e-reader out, the backlight shining on his face. Apparently, whatever he was reading was hilarious.

At the far end, the only other woman, Raine Josephs, snored quietly. Maria lay down on her bedroll and looked at the hazy sky, the stars obscured by smoke from the wildfire that had flared to life the day before.

Somewhere out there, her father was being held captive.

Years in the CIA hadn't given her a lead as to who was responsible. The men who had shot her mother in front of her and then taken her father from her went unpunished because she hadn't ever managed to find their identities. Only evidence that her father had been used for his skills and then sold to someone else. The first transaction in a chain she'd been able to track. Always one step behind actually finding him.

This personal mission had driven her ever since. It had led to her capture in Syria, where she'd come face-to-face with the enemy. At the time, she hadn't known who he was—outside of her personal connection to him. Her *asset*.

Despite the Trouble Boys not wanting her to be his target again, she'd found out what she needed to know about who the man was. And what he had done.

Three weeks after her capture, she'd been rescued by a Delta Force unit who'd been betrayed by people who should've had their backs. All because their teammate had sold them out, they'd landed in a mission that nearly got them all killed.

These men had fought for her.

Stuck with her.

Called her family.

They'd never given up.

Maria swiped tears from her face. Their fight had become hers. Her fight had become theirs.

If she didn't figure out how to finish it soon, she could lose them all.

Day seven hundred thirteen of being dead started like any other day. Kane Foster tied the laces on his boots and didn't bother to run his hands through his hair. It wasn't like there was a mirror out here.

He glanced at Mack. "Ready?"

The kid was twenty as of last week, and finally quit texting long enough to realize Kane was talking to him. "What—yep, ready." He unfolded those wiry limbs and stood, his features darker than his older brother Hammer.

"How is Alexis today?" Who else would the kid be texting other than a certain young woman he'd met last summer?

Mack eyed him. "How is Sanchez?"

Kane shoved his shoulder. "Bet you can't beat me to the trailhead." He swiped up his pack and took off running west, to the spot where the others had gathered. The carb-loaded breakfast sat heavy in his stomach, but he would need all the energy for the day. He hadn't lied to Sanchez about that.

Mack caught up, his dark eyes and long lashes far too knowing. "Alexis is fine, by the way."

"Good. She's at the teens camp?"

"Wildlands Academy, yeah." Mack nodded. "She said they took a field trip and fought a fire from a train with a water tank car. They rode the train and sprayed the fire."

"And now you wanna put out a fire from a train?"

Mack glanced over. "Don't you?"

"Okay, fair point," Kane said. "That would be cool."

"She also found out she got a job as an EMT in Bozeman, so she's moving in a couple of weeks."

"Tell her I said well done, yeah?"

Mack nodded, and Kane spotted the pinch of frustration at the edge of his expression. The kid had met Alexis last year in Montana. She was the daughter of a buddy of theirs, a firefighter from Last Chance County who'd joined the Ember crew as a hotshot. One of the smokejumpers here in Alaska, Orion Price, was Alexis's half brother. Mack had earned a lot of respect—and it was probably why Charlie let the kid text with his daughter.

Kane said, "Patience is a good thing. Same with not being reckless when the most likely outcome is that someone gets hurt."

Mack walked beside him to the trailhead, over the uneven, rocky ground normally traversed by four-legged creatures. Not so many two-legged, except them. "Still sucks."

"But it's the right thing. She might be eighteen now, but she's still young." Kane reached over and squeezed the back of the kid's neck. "You know where she is when the time is right."

"Pretty sure it'll be right as soon as the season is done. If the mission is finished then."

"I get you." Kane chuckled. "And I hope the mission is finished as well. Being dead is getting old."

They caught up to the rest of the hotshots and started the hike to the fire line.

Kane's phone buzzed in his pocket. It was almost as if thinking about family connections had summoned a text from his cousin in Last Chance County.

Kane would have to wait until less people were around before reading and responding to it, something Ridge knew well enough. His cousin never called. He let Kane call him when he could do it without anyone knowing. Even if it didn't matter that these people knew he and Ridge were related.

What mattered was that the world kept believing Kane, Hammer, and Saxon were dead.

Juggling all the secrets was becoming tiresome. Although, his feelings for Sanchez weren't a secret. Everyone knew how he felt about her, and most of the people they worked with presumed she felt the same about him. But the need to maintain focus and not cross any lines meant he worked hard to compartmentalize it all. She would never be *Maria*. She would always be *Sanchez*.

Once he tumbled off that cliff, it would be a long way down. Kane would never get back up.

Kind of like Mack with the young woman he'd fallen for, the timing had to be right.

Still, Kane had never been a fan of "yes but not yet" from the Lord.

Waiting sucked as much as having to search locations one by one, eliminating each in turn. Narrowing down the search for her father. The search for a canister of dangerous toxin their enemy—the man who had betrayed his team—wanted to use to destabilize the US.

Mack jogged up to walk beside his brother, Hammer. Saxon chatted with Raine, the two of them walking beside each other.

Grizz and Mitch were in the lead.

Sanchez stepped off to the side and looked at the sky. She'd pulled her dark hair back today, and it shone in the morning sun. High cheekbones. A slender figure but with so much strength packed into it from fighting wildfires that it sometimes seemed like she could withstand anything. When he'd caught up to her, she joined him at the back of the line. Like it was no big deal to stop and wait for him. Almost like she wanted to be near him.

Kind of like the way he wanted to be near her.

"So where are we headed today?" He didn't glance at her. *Play it cool and no one gets burned.*

"Because you weren't listening to the briefing, you were talking to Mack?" She motioned to the kid, up ahead, tossing rocks off the trail every twenty feet or so.

Really? The kid was just walking through the backcountry, chucking rocks like this was a stroll?

Kane focused back on Maria—and caught the disgruntled look on her face. He chuckled. "Hit me with the highlights."

She kept pace with him, her strength clearer in the lines of her muscles now than it had been when they met. She'd always been strong, but the physical nature of this work had brought a lot more of that strength to the surface.

It was enough to make a guy think he had heart problems.

If the woman ever dressed up to go out, he wasn't sure he'd survive.

"The North Fire is zero-percent contained. It's headed for a thirty-acre patch of trees that got infested with some bug that ate them all from the inside out. There's no moisture and a bunch of dry tinder. If the fire swallows that, it'll grow, and the whole place will go up like a barn full of hay."

"Is that right?"

She shoved his shoulder. "I can speak backcountry."

"You were born in San Diego."

"There are farms there!"

Kane busted up laughing. "Sure, sure."

"And I'm supposed to believe you're a regular blue-collar guy from Last Chance County? Because I've met more than one of those the past couple of years, and you're . . . something different."

"Is that right?"

"Commendations. Medals. The only reason you don't have a Purple Heart is because you're supposedly dead."

"Mmm. Shame." He rolled his shoulders, more of a reflex than anything else. "I don't want recognition over what happened. This is far from done."

But in his heart and mind, he had to acknowledge it, because he knew better than anyone that ignoring stuff or burying it just meant more trouble later.

Their team had been betrayed.

"You don't want a medal because you think it was your fault." She glanced aside at him. "Even though it wasn't. You guys were there to rescue me. You had no idea—"

"Neither did you," Kane said.

"So neither of us is at fault."

"We've been over this."

Sanchez sighed. "You rescued me, and you were betrayed."

"Now ask me what we'd have done if we knew going in that it was a trap. So I can tell you we'd have done it anyway. We'd have rescued you even if we knew it would work out like this."

She shook her head but said nothing.

"And when Hammer realized Mack was at home, living under his father's thumb—the worst kind of place to be—we picked him up and brought him with us. Because we don't let people fall through the cracks. Everyone deserves to have someone show up for them. You, me, and Mack."

He continued, "Now we're going to do the same with your father. And we're going to find the people behind the Sons of Revolution militia and finish this. When it's all done, we're going to get our lives back."

"I hope so." She said it so quietly he almost didn't hear it.

The line of hotshots slowed, and Mitch stepped off the trail, toward the tree line.

"I guess we're here." Kane knew for a fact there was a snowcapped mountain in front of them, but the thick wildfire smoke made it invisible. Enclosed them in a cloud that hung like fog on the horizon and caused a scratch in his throat that he had to cough out.

Saxon walked back to them. "Everything okay?"

Kane and Saxon had been in boot camp together. They'd fought, sweated, and bled together. Now they were dead together. It brought a certain clarity to everything he did. Who had time to beat around the bush when the fate of a country was on the line?

"Everything is fine. What's with the location?" Kane motioned up the trail and spotted Mack right as he tossed another rock.

He knew Saxon didn't buy that he was fine, but he didn't challenge Kane. "Mitch said there's a cabin through the—"

An explosion rocked the ground under them. Fire, smoke, and dirt sprayed into the air, caught a tree and sent it skyward in pieces.

All of them ducked into a crouch.

The last one down was Raine, looking around at him and Saxon. "What was that?"

"No one move!" Everything in Kane went cold. "That was a land mine."

AKNOWLEDGEMENTS

I'm so thankful to Susan May Warren and Lisa Phillips for putting this project together. I'm so honored to be a part of Chasing Fire: Alaska. I've loved being a part of Sunrise Publishing and this project was so much fun. Thanks to my friends, family, and co-workers that have supported me with my crazy busy schedule and encouraging me with my writing. I couldn't have done it without you! Thanks to my friends in the writing community. I love how supportive and encouraging other writers are, and I've been blessed with wonderful friendships, prayer warriors, and brainstorming partners. Thanks to all of the readers I've had the privilege of meeting over the past few years. Thank you for taking a chance on my stories and I hope to continue entertaining and delighting readers for years to come.

Kelly Underwood's favorite things are reading, writing, and drinking coffee. She was born in New Hampshire, but don't ask her about snow, because she's been a Florida girl since she was twelve. She writes book reviews for her blog bestinsuspense. com and is an active member of the Central Florida chapter of the American Christian Fiction Writers. She's a sucker for a good suspense novel, the kind you have to read cover-to-cover until the mystery is solved and the bad guys are in handcuffs. If you're looking for her, she's probably on her back patio with a Kindle in one hand and a cup of coffee in the other. Visit Kelly at kellyunderwoodauthor.com

DIVE INTO AN EPIC JOURNEY IN BOOK ONE OF
CHASING FIRE: MONTANA

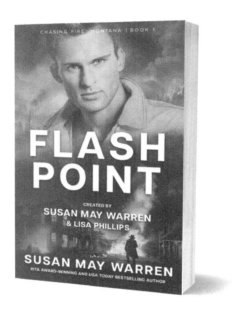

The Hollywood heartthrob and the firefighter with a secret...

What could go wrong?

Available on Amazon

LAST CHANCE
FIRE AND RESCUE

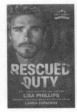   

USA Today Bestselling Author

LISA PHILLIPS

with **LAURA CONAWAY**, **MEGAN BESING** and **MICHELLE SASS ALECKSON**

The men and women of the Last Chance County Fire Department struggle to put a legacy of corruption behind them. They face danger every day on the job as first responders, but the fight to become a family will be their biggest battle yet. When hearts are on the line it's up to each one to trust their skill and lean on their faith to protect the ones they love. Before it all goes down in flames.

WE THINK YOU'LL ALSO LOVE...

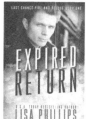

Fire Department liaison Allen Frees may have put his life back together, but getting the truck crew and engine squad to succeed might be his toughest job yet. When a child is nearly kidnapped, Allen steps in to help Pepper Miller keep her niece safe. The one thing he couldn't fix was the love he lost, but he isn't going to let Pepper walk away this time.

Expired Return by Lisa Phillips

Stunt double Vienna Foxcroft's stunt team are the only ones she trusts. Then in walks Sergeant Crew Gatlin and his tough-as-nails military dog, Havoc. When an attack on a film set sends them fleeing into the streets of Turkey, Vienna must face the demons of her past or be devoured by them. And Crew and Havoc will be tested like never before.

Havoc by Ronie Kendig

When an attempt is made on Grey Parker's life and dead bodies begin piling up, suddenly bodyguard Christina Sherman is tasked with keeping both a soldier and his dog safe... and with them, the secrets that could stop a terrorist attack.

Driving Force by Lynette Eason and Kate Angelo

We solve the problem of what we read next.   Available on Amazon

sunrise
PUBLISHING

**WHERE EVERY STORY IS A FRIEND,
AND EVERY CHAPTER IS A NEW JOURNEY...**

Subscribe to our newsletter for a free book, the latest news, weekly giveaways, exclusive author interviews, and more!

follow us on social media!

 @sunrisemediagroup

 @sunrisepublish

 @sunrisepublishing

Made in United States
Cleveland, OH
26 July 2025